Spring Break in Dubai with A Gangsta

A. Ward

Chapter 1

Memori

"So, is he the reason we aren't making love anymore? Has our situation really gotten that bad that we can't address our problems with one another? This shit is unbelievable. You would rather go confide in another motherfucking man who knows nothing about you, me, or us. I'm your fucking husband, Memori. If you got a problem, bring that shit to me."

Growing rather tired of his accusations, I sat back in my seat, listening to my husband rant and rave about the message thread he found in my iPhone between myself and my therapist. I allowed the bickering to continue, feeling justified in my reasoning for ignoring his nonsense. I'd done no wrong and wasn't at any fault. He's my therapist; it was his job to hear my problem and diagnose what the best course of action was. As my husband continued to piss me off, I finally hit my boiling point and interrupted his annihilation of my character.

"Nigel, it's not that serious. He's just my therapist. There's nothing going on between the two of us. If you would've read the messages and not skimmed through the thread, you would've seen that. Besides, I needed to get some things off my chest that you just wouldn't and still won't listen to."

"I won't listen?" he uttered. "Bit... When? When have you come to me with any of these things that I'm reading?"

"Don't do that, Nigel. I always try to come to you first." Nigel placed his hands on his hips and glared at me with the same look he'd give our children when they'd fucked up.

"Don't do what?" he spat.

"Don't look at me like I'm one of our children. I'm a grown ass woman, and if we're going to talk, let's act accordingly." He fixed his posture, and I continued with my statement. "As I was saying, there's nothing in those messages that should be news to you. Every single thing that I've told him is the same thing I've come to you about in some way, shape, form, or fashion. We've had issues in our marriage for a while, yet anytime I bring my concerns to you, you just brush me off and place me on your list of things to do. I'm your fucking wife. I shouldn't be categorized with your calendar, objectified and squeezed into dates in your phone."

"Memori, I don't give a damn what you say. If it was that big of a deal to you, you would have made me sit down and listen. Hell, you do it when you need money. You did it about the dumb ass trip to Dubai you and your girls are taking. You do it when you need them stupid ass Malaysian bundles. Why the fuck do I keep having to fork out two to four hundred dollars every two weeks so you can walk around with an Asian woman's skull cap? All that shit coming from your lips right now sound like bullshit because you got caught. Your mouth is moving with little substance right now, but these messages, right here in black and white, show me something completely different. There's more to y'all than what you're saying. You aren't about to toy with me, woman. As of right now, I'll play your game and give you the benefit of the doubt, but if I'm going to keep paying for these stupid ass therapy sessions, you need to find a new therapist. This one isn't working out."

It was like a bad scene from *Waiting to Exhale*. I folded my arms and bit my lip, refraining from speaking the words that were brewing in my mind. Nigel's insecurities were frustrating me and quite honestly, I was beyond tired of being the victim of his mental problems. His mental issues were the reason I was seeing a therapist in the first place. Day in and day out, I felt that there were new issues with him. If I wore my hair a certain way, there was a problem. I couldn't smile a certain way without him accusing me of thinking of another man. I guess in his eyes, I was supposed to be the trophy wife, but his vision for that role seemed more like me being a fucking robot, which I was not. He toyed around with my phone for a few more minutes before breaking his silence again and handing it back to me.

"You don't have to worry about texting him anymore. His number has been deleted from your phone. I'll be contacting his office in the morning to make sure that they won't be scheduling any more visits." He stated angrily.

I sat there, shaking my head in disbelief, scrolling through my call logs and texts. Nigel had done exactly what he said. I needed a moment as I took a deep breath and rolled my eyes to myself.

"If that's what you want, dear husband, you've got it. I don't know how many more ways and times I must show you that I ain't doing shit. You keep accusing me of doing shit, but if it's that big of a deal, you can come to the next session with me, which is tomorrow, and explain to my therapist why I won't be coming back to see him. Hell, it's not like I haven't been trying to get you to come anyway, but again, it's always placed on that list of things to do for you, or it's, 'I'll get back to you and let you know.'"

It must have struck a nerve within him. "You not fucking going. That's final!" he yelled, storming out of our bedroom, breathing heavily, mumbling obscene gestures under his breath. He slammed the door with so much force, he shook one of the pictures off the wall, breaking it as it hit the floor.

I sat on the edge of our bed, trying to find a way to restore my messages. I'd made a mental note of the things he'd said to me, so that I could keep them locked away for tomorrow's session. As I continued to sit in solitude, I caught a glimpse of Nigel backing out of the driveway. It had begun to rain, but he was so pissed, he was going to weather the storm. He had his music turned up so loud, I could hear every word playing through the speaker crystal clear.

> *First off fuck yo' bitch and the clique you claim*
>
> *Westside when we ride come equipped with game*
>
> *You claim to be a player, but I fucked yo' wife*
>
> *We bust on Bad Boys niggas fucked for life.*

Tupac was coming word for word at me, and it further solidified the fact that he couldn't handle the truth. Anytime Nigel felt anger or rage, he'd listen to gangster rap music and try to mimic the persona. To some people, it may have worked, but I saw right through his facade. It was hard not to, especially knowing him the way that I did. He was nothing more than a cupcake. He was my cupcake, but a cupcake, nonetheless. He was once a sweet, loving, caring man. He used to listen to me and cater to my needs up until that damn promotion at his job. The number of hours he started working increased, and he began to get a big head because people had to look up at him as a boss, which further turned him into a monster. His entire attitude changed. So did the way he dealt with people, especially me. I was a victim of his rage and attempting to be a loving, supportive, understanding wife, I allowed him to tear the woman that I was down. My sessions were my way of coping with the monster he'd become and reminding myself that he could go back to the old him, but he was attempting to strip that access away from me as well.

An hour or so passed, and I'd finally gained the strength to pry myself from my place on our California King bed. I made my way into our massive kitchen and cracked open the wine cabinet. Placing a glass on the island, I grabbed a bottle of '96 Dom Pérignon, filled the glass to the rim, and walked into the living room. I tucked myself under one of my favorite throw pillows, before turning the television on. There was nothing that sparked my interest as I flipped through the channels. Ultimately, I decided that some music would be the perfect way to escape the sad reality I was living in and put my mind at ease. With the weather the way it was, I was hopeful that it could change my attitude at the very least. I took a sip from the glass then accidentally spilled some on our white Persian rug. "Fuck!" I yelled, placing one of the throw pillows over my face. Once I was able to get the yelling out of my system, I looked up towards the cathedral ceiling and allowed the music to serenade my soul. I sat, teary-eyed, singing word for word.

I told myself that I would make some changes

but the more I change, there's one thing that remains the same.

I can't seem to shake ya

you seem to really have a hold on me

and every time that we break up

we turn around and make up.

The smooth, sweet sounds of Destiny's Child played, and I felt every word sang in the song. Their harmonizing voices were speaking to me. I was stonger than I was leading myself on to believe. Every single lyric resonated with my current situation. I didn't know if it was a sign from above, but for the moment, I was thankful that someone in the universe could relate to how I was feeling. My phone began to buzz as the song continued, and it was a text from an unfamiliar number.

Hey, I hope that your day is going well. I'm sure you been the source of a smile somewhere and if not, you have by reading this. I just wanted to speak some positivity into your day as well as make sure that we were still on for our session tomorrow?

-S.V.

I smiled for the first time seemingly all day and read the message twice. It was from my therapist, Dr. Sincere Valentino. He was such a sweet guy and knew how to turn shit into sugar in the simplest of ways.

My day could be better, but I won't complain. I must take the good with the bad. Thank you for the source of positivity. It really helped make my day at least one percent better. As far as the session tomorrow, I am going out on a limb to say yes but it may be my last one. My husband isn't fond of the way we do things with the texting and all so he may be there tomorrow. Fingers crossed. This may have been the breakdown that leads to the breakthrough for him.

-Memori

I exhaled after typing the message. The timing of the text coming through when it did seemed to be another sign from the universe. My therapist was the release point I needed with the amount of tension the day brought on me. He was my go-to when all else failed. I didn't have very many friends. The ones I did have were separated from me when Nigel decided to move us out of the city, placing us square in the boondocks. The few people I did consider friends weren't the type to blend in with our new lifestyle, and a couple of them went as far as to tell me that they felt I'd become exactly like the people we moved close to. Besides my best friend, Tiffany, I had no one to vent to, and Sincere was my one constant.

Well, I hope that he makes the right decision and joins us. I don't want him to think that he isn't welcomed or that our sessions are anything but professional. I will do my best to put him at ease with the situation and hopefully by the end, he will change his mind about things. If he isn't ok with that, I will gladly sit down with him and talk out whatever problem there seems to be.

-S.V.

"Where were the guys like him when I was dating?" I thought aloud. He was willing to stand up to my husband for me and have an awkward conversation when he didn't have to. That itself showed me that he was serious about making sure that I was ok at all costs.

You don't have to do that. Thank you for the offer. It's good to know that there are still some good guys in the world, and that you would do that for me. I think that we will play it by ear and go from there at the session if he shows. I will let you get back to work because I know you have other clients to take care of besides me, so I will see you in the morning.

-Memori

He responded with one last message, and it was as sweet of a gesture as he could make.

Jusque la', belle. Prends soin (Until then, beautiful. Take care)

-S.V.

I placed my phone on the coffee table and sipped what was left of the glass of wine I'd poured myself. I said a prayer in hopes that it would be answered. It was simple one. I could only hope that Nigel would join me for my therapy session, just to see the genuine nature Sincere had. However, knowing Nigel, I figured it wouldn't happen, and my prayer would fall on deaf ears.

Morning came and as expected, Nigel decided that it would be a good idea to stay out drinking for most of the night. He flopped down on the bed in the same filthy clothes he had on the day before, waking me up. The sun beamed through the window, making beautiful rays through the satin curtains. I knew that he would be too hungover to get up, so I took it upon myself to be rather petty, considering the situation. I leaned over and kissed his ears, hoping that he would be just coherent enough for me to piss him off.

"Good morning, baby. Wake up. I need you," I moaned gently in his ear.

He grunted and shrugged his shoulders but never lifted his body from the bed nor did he open his eyes.

"Baby, wake up. I have something I need to tell you," I

insisted, running my hand over his chest, slowly inching towards his belt buckle. I could feel his blood rushing and his manhood beginning to throb. Placing a single kiss on his lips, which still tasted like liquor, I heard him moan. His breath was atrocious, but that didn't stop me from having my fun. Besides, everybody knew that drunk dick was the best dick. If I was going to be subjected to his way of doing things, I was going to find a way to please myself in the meantime. I was able to get his belt loose and unzip his pants. As I reached into his boxers, something about him felt different. I pulled his dick out, the dick that belonged to me, and anger set in.

"What the fuck?" I mumbled? "Nigel, wake the fuck up! What the hell is this?" I was in true disbelief. "Nigel. I know you fucking hear me. Wake the fuck up." I retracted my hand after feeling the rubber still attached to the foreskin of his dick. "Get the fuck up!" I yelled once more before slapping his chest.

His eyes were barely opened as he placed one of his hands over them, blocking the glare from the sun. "What the fuck, woman? Don't you see I'm trying to sleep? What the fuck is wrong with you now?" he questioned still in a trance.

I was hurt. I got so pissed off that I couldn't speak. I took the open palm of my hand and conjured as much power as I could to slap his face.

"What the fuck is wrong with you?" he questioned, this time springing up from the bed to protect his face.

He must have felt the breeze hit his dick as he looked down and noticed the rubber hanging.

"Oh shit," he stated, chasing behind me.

I rushed out of the bedroom with a face full of tears. Grabbing my car keys, I made my way to the car. He had me so distraught, I dropped the keys on the floorboard. Once I picked them up, my hands were shaking so bad, I couldn't even place them in the ignition. It took me several moments to gather enough composure to finally do so. I looked up towards the front door and noticed Nigel stumbling, trying to get out of it, fixing his pants. He stopped and leaned against the frame of it, motioning for me to come back inside. I threw up my middle finger, put the car in reverse, and drove away. I tried to call my best friend, Tiffany, but she didn't answer. With the sunshine beaming through my windshield, I realized that she was probably fast asleep. She worked third shift and was usually out like a light around this time. With nowhere else to turn, I made the decision to head straight for my therapist's office earlier than he would be expecting me.

Chapter 2

Sincere

"Good morning, Dr. Valentino," Shianne, my receptionist and fiancée, spoke as she did every morning in my passing her to head into my office.

"Bonjour," I replied seductively, flirting with her with my accent.

I walked over to the coffee pot and poured myself a cup before starting my day. I winked at Shianne as I headed into my office with my briefcase in one hand and coffee in the other. Shianne sprung up from her seat, and I could sense something strange was going on. She rushed over to me, making me spill a little bit of my coffee on to my blazer, shirt, and tie.

"Shit," I uttered as the hot coffee began to seep through. "Everything good, baby?" I questioned. Something about her seemed off. She grabbed a paper towel and began trying to help clean some of the mess she made.

"I am so sorry, Dr. Valentino," she stated flabbergasted.

"It's ok. It's not that big of a deal, but is something on your mind?" I questioned, removing the blazer, taking the towel from her.

"Yes…well, no… Yes, but please don't be upset."

"What's going on, Shianne? You're never this off in the morning. Usually, I have to jump on you about snapping pictures on your cell phone, but you not even doing that, so what is it?"

"Ok, hey, before you go in. One of your clients is here early. She's extremely upset, so I didn't want to just turn her away. I went ahead and let her in. I hope I didn't overstep my boundaries."

I was caught off guard by the suddenness but understood what she explained. Placing my blazer over my forearm, I entered my office suite. Much to my surprise, it was my patient, Memori Stills. Her face was soaked with the moisture from her tears. I placed my belongings on the top of my desk and made my way over to the chaise lounge that she was sitting on. I placed one arm around her and pulled her into me, allowing her to drain the rest of her emotions. Although it was against many of the founding principles established between therapist and patient, it was apparent that she needed a shoulder to cry on.

It took a few minutes, but I was able to calm her nerves down enough to get her to speak. I wiped the tears from her eyes and handed her a tissue from the box sitting on the edge of my desk.

"Mrs. Stills, what's going on? Our appointment wasn't until later this morning. What's happened that's brought you into my office almost three hours earlier than anticipated?"

She began to find her emotions once again as she began to speak through a crackled voice.

"I'm so sorry, Dr. Valentino. I just didn't know where else to go. I thought I could fix it, but I can't."

"Fix what, Memori? What's going on?"

"Him. It's just him. My husband. He's cheating on me. I just thought we were having marital issues, but he's actually cheating on me. I've been nothing but good to this man. Even with all the shit he's accused me of, I've remained nothing but loyal, and this is what he does to me."

She broke down once more, and I found myself consoling her

yet again. I placed my hand on her back, attempting to ease the pain she was feeling.

"This is not on you, understand that. You've done everything that you can to be the woman that he needs. Process it, live through the emotions, and come out stronger. This doesn't define the woman you are, but rather the man he is."

As I concluded my statement, Shianne walked into the office, grabbing my attention.

"Hey, Dr. Valentino, I know that you have a client, but we have someone in the lobby looking to speak to you, and it seems rather urgent," she spat as I heard a man yell in the waiting area.

"Sit here. I'll be right back," I spoke gently to Memori.

Making my way into the waiting area, I noticed the rather large gentleman with shades covering his eyes. His clothing was wrinkled and stained. As I approached the gentleman, he removed his glasses.

"You S.V.? You the motherfucker fucking up my marriage, texting my wife all this bullshit?"

"Pardon me," I voiced with concern.

"Dr. Valentino, right? You the nigga that's been texting my wife. Yeah, you didn't think I would find out. Well, I'm just here to let you know face to face that you won't be seeing her anymore. I know she has an appointment with you later today, but she won't make it."

I was confused as to who the gentleman's wife was. Before he had a chance to mention a name, I looked over at my fiancée and shared a chuckle with her.

"Sir, I don't know who your wife is without a names or any other information. Even if I did, my patient confidentiality clause would prevent me from digging into this conversation with you right here right now. So as calmly as I can, I'm asking you to leave my practice."

"I ain't going nowhere, nigga. That shit with you and Memori ends today."

Hearing Memori's name triggered me. It was all coming full circle to me who the man was.

"Mr. Stills is it? I hate that we have to meet you under these circumstances, however, I assure you that whatever issue you have with my communication with your wife, it's not what you think it is. I apologize about us getting off on the wrong foot, so let's start again. It's a pleasure to meet you."

Extending my hand was my attempt to try to put away any ill feelings, but my hand was met with a disrespectful slap back at me.

"I ain't shaking yo' fucking hand, nigga. You must think this is a game or something. You are fucking my wife, or at least wanting to. I know how you clown ass niggas get down. Y'all try to sweet talk y'all's way into these innocent women's panties. You niggas fuck with their minds to get them open, then try to get some pussy from them. You ain't about to get Memori, my nigga. She mine. You hear me? She mine."

The liquor was strong on his breath, and he was premeditating his move. I watched his clenched fist move towards my face as he attempted to swing on me.

"Wow. I will let the ill-advised swing go due to your drunken nature, sir." I adjusted my shirt and looked him dead in the eyes. "With all due respect, I'm not attempting to do anything with your wife. The last thing that I would ever make her out to be is a cheater, unlike yourself. I'm not that type of man. Now with all that, Mr. Stills, again, I can't speak for other practices, but that's not how I conduct business. I promise you, nothing but professionalism is happening between your wife and myself. Considering your actions, I'm going to have to ask you to leave, as my other clients are starting to arrive. If you'd like, you can come back at the time of your wife's appointment this afternoon, and we can all can chat, or you can set up a private appointment for yourself, and we can defuse the negative connotation you have on the situation."

"Yeah, aight. That shit sounds good."

The tension in the room was running high and compounded further as my office door swung open. An awkward silence filled the room. Not a word was uttered as Memori and Nigel stared at one another. Shianne coughed, breaking the silence in the room. Nigel broke the glare and looked at me.

"Ain't shit going on, huh? This hoe running back to you, reporting our problems?"

I placed one hand on my forehead before I walked over to Memori, attempting to get her back into my office. Nigel's words were like a flame to a match as they lit a fuse on a bomb that was ready to explode.

"Hoe? So now your wife, who you claim to love, is a hoe in your eyes? Really, Nigel? I wasn't the one with a condom attached to me. That was your bitch ass this morning."

I motioned for Shianne to move the other clients of mine into another room as I attempted to diffuse the situation that was before me.

"You two, my office now," I stated, walking towards the door.

"Nah, fuck that shit. You can keep this hoe; I'm out!" Nigel, barked turning towards the door to leave.

"Running from the problem isn't going to help, Mr. Stills," I mentioned, hoping to get him to come back to talk the issues out.

He raised his hand with the middle finger pointed in our direction and continued out the door. A few moments later, a loud crashing sound echoed from outside. I looked out the window, and so did Memori. He'd taken a brick and busted one of her windows out.

"I'm about to kill this man." She reached into her purse and pulled out a blade before running towards the door.

"No. No, Memori, I can't let you do that. If I allow you to go stab him, you end up going to jail. I can't allow that to happen."

"What am I supposed to do? I have to go back home and live with this monster?"

"Let me think." I contemplated for a second on what I had available to me that could possibly help her. "When is your trip to Dubai scheduled?"

"I leave in three days. Why? What does that have to do with anything?"

I walked over to my briefcase on my desk and pulled out a card. It was to the manager of the Watermark hotel in Baton Rouge.

"Call this number and tell him it's a favor for me. If he has any questions, tell him to call me directly. This should at least get you away from your husband for a couple days until your trip, or at least until you both have cooled down enough to talk to one another."

She looked at the card, and her eyes got teary again.

"Thank you," she spoke as she got up from her seat and hugged me before heading out.

As she exited, I wasn't too far behind her. I walked into my lobby and looked over at Shianne. I knew that I was up shit's creek without a paddle because the look on her face said that she wasn't happy with me. I put on the fakest smile I could and greeted my clients that had to sit through that entire fiasco.

"Please forgive everything that you all saw here today.

Today's session is free of charge. Please follow me."

I escorted them into my office and went on about the rest of my day.

Chapter 3

Memori

A few hours passed and I found myself sitting outside of my best friend's apartment. I didn't want to go bother her knowing that she was sleep, but I didn't have anywhere else to go. The hotel that Dr. Valentino set me up with wouldn't allow me to check in until after 3 p.m., and that was even with an early check in. I couldn't believe how bad things truly had gotten with me and Nigel. We'd had differences before, but it had never gotten to this point. I looked over at the busted passenger side window and wept.

An Amazon truck pulled up and rang the doorbell to Tiffany's apartment. A couple moments passed, and she came to the door with her robe undone, not covering any parts of her body, exposing undergarments. She looked like she was trying to get the attention of the Amazon driver but had missed him. In her sight, she caught a glimpse of me sitting there.

"Memori!" she yelled as she motioned for me. I got out of the car and headed towards her door.

"What are you doing here, girl? Why are your eyes red? You been crying? What's wrong?"

In the midst of her slew of questions, I broke down on her doorstep.

"On no, girl, get in here."

She ushered me into her house and covered herself up. She

had a stick of sage burning, a blunt in an ashtray, and Erykah Badu playing in her apartment.

"Excuse the mess, I was cleansing my spirits and healing my soul."

I sat down on the couch, and she brought me a glass of water.

"So, talk to me girl, what's going on?"

I took a sip from the glass and began to explain to her what my issue was.

"It's Nigel. He just caused an entire scene at my therapist's office. He thought that I was fucking around with my therapist, and this entire time, he was the one cheating."

Tiffany took a deep breath and tried to comprehend what was just thrown her way.

"So, let me unpack this. You finally got him to go to therapy with you, and he had the audacity to think you were fucking what's his name? I mean, that man is fine. Shit, I'd fuck him."

She managed to turn my bad situation into something that I could laugh about for a moment. That's why I loved her. She was true to herself and always knew how to make a bad situation better.

"Sincere is his name, but essentially, yes. He went through my phone and saw some text messages and made that assumption.

Tiffany picked up her blunt and sparked it while inhaling a large puff.

"How do you know he was cheating?"

"We had an argument last night. Just typical shit with him lately. He came home drunk this morning, and you know drunk dick has that added umph to it, so I wanted to get off and was hoping that it would take the edge off the tension between the both of us. Make up sex, you know? I reached into his pants to pull out his dick, and this nigga still had a condom on it."

I began to cry, telling her the story, but I was all teared out.

"I know you fucking lying. Girl, fuck Nigel. He hasn't been right since that job told him he was somebody and added a couple of zeros to his paycheck. He ain't shit, ain't gone be shit. Hell, for all I know, fuck his mama too for raising that piece of shit."

"Then, at the office, he busted my window out. It's been a long couple of days."

Tiffany inhaled another puff of her blunt then reached out to hand it to me. I waved her off, but she was insistent on me taking a puff.

"Here, bitch, you need this more than I do. It'll relax you and take your mind off that bullshit. I really can't believe that after all this time together, he would think you would step out on him. I mean, shit, you've held this nigga down through a lot of shit. There is no fucking way he can truly be this dumb, and then to cheat. I just can't. Well, look, bitch, you can crash here. The kids left with their daddy earlier than expected for spring break, so I got room.

"I have a hotel that my therapist set me up with. I'm going to take advantage of that before our trip. Thank you for the offer, though."

"You know you my girl. I got you for life. I love you."

She got up from her seat and came to sit next to me. She gave me a big hug and kissed my forehead. No matter what, Tiffany was the true definition of ride or die.

"Now since you got this room situation on lock, I'ma go pack a bag because I'm coming to stay with you at this hotel. I need to see something other than these four walls, and since our flight doesn't leave for Dubai for a few more days, this is the perfect opportunity for me to get into vacation mode. Okuuurrrdddd!"

She stuck her tongue out and was dead ass serious as she walked to the back of her apartment and gathered some of her clothing and personal items. As she did, my phone began to ring. It was Nigel. I ignored his back-to-back calls before he texted me.

Look, I'm sorry. I'll get the car window fixed. I lost control of my emotions. Please come home so that we can talk.

-Nigel

I debated for a moment as I read the text, but I'd had enough. For once, I needed to do what was in the best interest of myself. Tiffany made that decision a lot easier as she had her things ready in no time.

"Girl, why are you still sitting down? I'm ready to go."

I looked at her, and the two of us shared a laugh.

"I am too, but the hotel won't let me check in until after three."

She took off her bonnet and flopped back down into the recliner adjacent from me.

"You know how to take the wind out a bitch sails," she stated, sounding disappointed. "Oh, we should call Summer and Monica and see if they want to come to the hotel too. Just start vacation right now."

"Now you know Summer's stuck-up ass isn't going to be down to stay with us in a hotel. At least not in the city anyway. With her getting that big ass mansion, after her divorce settlement, she might not leave the house again and you know it's a strong chance that Monica will cancel on us last minute. I've been waiting for the text from her for a few days," I responded.

Right on cue, both of our phones went off with a text from

Monica in our girl group chat.

Ladies, I cannot wait for this trip. It is much needed. I am so excited and can't wait to see my girls. I miss you all lots. -Monica

"As you were saying," Tiffany came back and mentioned.

I shook my head at her and smiled.

"My answer is still no. I just want to relax, not stress, and have room service delivered to me."

Tiffany complied, and the two of us wasted time with small talk.

Chapter 4

Sincere

The ride home was silent. Shianne hadn't said a word, and neither had I. However, the tension grew thicker the closer we got to our home. Upon entering our living space, we made our way to the elevator, and I could feel a hole being stared into the side of my head. Shianne's constant huffing and puffing let me know that I was in far deeper than I could have even imagined.

"So, are we going to address the issue at hand, or are we brushing this one under the rug, Dr. Valentino?" Shianne questioned as the two of us made our way into the condo. She only called me Dr. Valentino when I'd done something she didn't like or when she was pissed off. In this instance, it was the combination of both. "I really thought that things would be different now that we are older, but some dogs just don't outgrow old tricks. Silly fucking me for believing that shit would really change."

I exhaled as I placed one hand over my head. I was stressed about the conversation that was to be had.

"Can we do this later, please? It's been a long enough day. The last thing the two of us need to do is dig deeper into this wound."

Shianne slammed her purse on the couch and walked ahead of me as the elevator doors opened.

"That shit ain't gone work, not this time. You aren't about to just blow this off. Why am I being blindsided by bullshit? I thought we were in this together, Sincere."

I took another deep breath, placing my blazer on the back of one of the dining room chairs. I proceeded to walk into the kitchen, and just like a shadow, Shianne was hot on my tail.

"Hello, I know you fucking hear me, Dr. Valentino."

Taking a glass from the cabinet, I poured myself a glass of scotch.

"Shianne, it's not that serious, and it's definitely not as deep as you're attempting to make this seem."

"Oh, but it is," she responded, taking the glass from my hands before sipping it for herself. "I shouldn't have to question your professionalism with clients. It's bad enough that there are stray bitches out in this world that would suck your dick for just looking their way, but bitches at our place of business? Un-fuckin'-believable. So let me ask, because her husband obviously has more insight and was extremely irate for just some professional talk. I can't believe that I even need to ask this. Did you fuck the bitch?"

"No… for goodness' sake, no. Do you really think that I would betray your trust like that? Really, Shianne?"

"Well, I didn't think you'd be texting this bitch behind my back, yet here we are. You got me smiling and greeting this hoe, letting her into the office early because she's having a mental fucking breakdown. So, what the fuck is up, Sincere, because it's obvious that something more is popping off here that I'm blind to."

I was growing more and more frustrated with her interrogation. The longer that I remained silent, the more fired up Shianne became. Her anger was turning into rage. She was pissed with me, hurt, yet still looking for me to formulate the reasoning behind my actions. Instead of finding an answer, I gave her more of what she'd been getting—silence. I got up from my seat and started walking away from her, undressing myself as I went.

"Are you fucking serious, Sincere? So, you still don't have an answer for me? NOTED!" Shianne yelled from the dining room.

I walked into the bedroom, plopping down on our king size bed. I placed a pillow over my head and yelled into it at the top of my lungs. Very little time passed before the bedroom door creaked open and Shianne appeared.

"Hi, it's me, you know, your partner in crime. The woman you claim to be the love of your life. I thought you might want to take this. It could be another one of them hoes we service."

I sat up on the bed and just looked at her as she held the phone midair while it vibrated uncontrollably.

"Whoever it is can wait," I responded.

"What the fuck ever!" Shianne exclaimed as she tossed the phone onto the bed and slammed the door.

I took a look at the phone as if it were nothing. It took me a few minutes, but I eventually looked at the missed call log and noticed it was an automated call from my bank, letting me know that my monthly wire transfer was completed.

I placed the phone down on my nightstand without responding and finished removing my clothes. I walked into the bathroom, starting the shower, hoping that it would help relax me and put me in a better head space. Once I got in and began to let the hot water trickle down my body, my peace was broken.

"Ready to talk now? Don't think this shit just gone get ignored, my boy. As a matter of fact," Shianne stopped mid-sentence and began to undress. "You think you about to have a peace of mind while I'm out here going through it, you got another thing coming. I'm getting in with you."

She reached into the shower to feel the temperature of the water and adjusted it to her liking.

"Shit!" I barked out as the water's temperature increased by at least ten degrees, burning my skin.

"What's wrong with you? Is it too hot? Get used to it. Hell is just as hot for lying motherfuckers like yourself."

She eased her way into the shower and stood in front of me, allowing the water to flow over her body, leaving me nothing but the cooler drops of water that fell off of her body.

I needed to put an end to the animosity. I was becoming fed up with the slick comments she was throwing my way and finally broke my silence on the matter. I turned Shianne around by the shoulder and looked into her eyes.

"Listen, and I mean listen as best as you can. I didn't fuck her and had no plans to fuck her. I haven't even said or made an advance sexually towards her. The most that I've said was, 'good morning, beautiful' or gave her some motivation to go about her day in a positive manner. That's it."

Shianne stared deep into my dark brown eyes and got a sense of relief.

"So why not say that instead of continuing to let the shit fester and build up on me? I don't like that about you, and you know that. That's that Aquarius bullshit."

"I didn't respond because I didn't feel the need to defend myself when you know me better than that, Shianne. Now come here and look at me. Really look at me. You are soon-to-be Mrs. Valentino. I'm not going to hide shit from you, and I hope the same can be expected in return. I love you."

She accepted my semi apology, and the two of us made up in the shower. Once we were finished and clean, we headed to the bed. Although there was nothing between Memori and I, I did feel concerned for her well-being and hoped that she was ok.

Chapter 5

Memori

The day arrived, as we were in the air on our way to Dubai. It had been a few days since Nigel and I had spoken. I managed to sneak back into the house while he was away at work to get packed the day before my vacation. I felt like it was lining up perfectly for me to get away without having the added stress of a fight. I did miss him, but I figured that we would talk once I got back from the much-needed vacation ahead of me.

"Ladies and gentlemen, please fasten your seatbelts; we are about to land," the captain spat over the plane's intercom system.

The plane came to a smooth landing, but we were stuck sitting, waiting for passengers to exit the plane for almost thirty minutes, but once we exited the plane, that anxious sigh of relief was exhaled.

"Ladies, we've made it," Tiffany yelled as we exited the concourse.

My girls and I stepped into the international airport, inhaling gasps of fresh air as we were no longer in America. We had arrived in Dubai.

"Yassssss, bitch! Now this is the shit I'm talking about," one of our other friends, Summer, stated.

The vibe was completely different here, and you could tell that from the atmosphere. Although the temperature was extremely warm, it was perfect compared to the on again, off again cycle we were going through back home in Louisiana. The sun kissed our brown skin as if it were molding us into bronze sculptures.

As we headed towards baggage claim, we managed to gain the attention of many travelers. Some looks were filled with astonishment, some were snobbish, but we didn't care; we were ready to have a good time and take Dubai by storm. One of the individuals whose attention we gained was a young man looking down at his phone. He walked over to us as he noticed us pulling things from the conveyor belt.

"Allow me to grab that for you, ma'am," the young gentleman's voice rang out with a deeply heavy accent. He reached out, attempting to grab my bag and I pulled it back abruptly.

"Excuse me, I don't know you," I blurted, swinging at him. We weren't even ten minutes in and I'd shown my ass in Dubai, it wasn't the initial impression that I wanted to leave on its natives, but I wasn't with any fuck shit either. "Please back the fuck away from me. I don't know you," I stated, making a scene in the middle of the area.

"Allow me to apologize for my suddenness. My name is Aquanis, and I'll be your tour guide for the rest of this week." He turned his phone towards us and showed us the itinerary that had been set up for us, along with our pictures. "Again, I apologize for the informal introduction and walking up so abruptly, but if you don't mind, please allow me to do my job."

He once again reached for my bag, and although not as harsh, I still rejected his assistance.

"I appreciate the gesture, but you don't have to do that!" I exclaimed to him.

My friends all turned to look at me then looked back up at Aquanis, who towered over all of us.

"Bitch… if you're not going to take this nice-looking man's

help, then I damn sure will," Tiffany responded, handing him her belongings.

I looked over at Aquanis and the smirk that he had on his face as he looked at Tiffany. The two of them locked eyes, and I could tell he was going to be trouble for her from that moment. He looked like he was up to no good. He'd gather everyone else's luggage, except mine. He did once again offer to grab my belongings, but again, I said no.

"I appreciate the offer again, but I'm a big girl. I can handle my own luggage. I carry my own weight.

He released a slight chuckle as he tipped his head and nodded toward me. He proceeded to carry what luggage he did collect like it was all light paper weight to him at one time.

Once he was done arranging the luggage that we had in the sprinter van, he opened the door to allow my friends and I in.

"Oh, this shit is nice," Monica, stated as she got comfortable in the van. "A little warm, but it's nice."

From the moment we stepped off the plane, one thing was obvious. Dubai was hot as hell.

"Hey, Aquanis, can we cut the air on in this motherfucker?" Tiffany asked.

"Tiffany, gawd damn. We ain't been here thirty minutes, and you already showing yo' ass. You don't have to be ratchet everywhere you go. Give the man a chance to get in the van himself, damn!" Summer exclaimed.

"My bad, man, you know how I get when I get hot."

"My apologies, once you have been here for so long, you get used to the heat," he replied before turning on the air.

As they went back and forth with one another, staying true to themselves, I was stuck knee deep in shit that I shouldn't have been in with Nigel.

I don't know why you aren't responding or answering the phone, but I know damn well that you're in Dubai by now. I need to hear from you asap.

-Nigel

It took me a few moments to go through every notification that my phone had coming through it, but I was finally able to and got back to responding to my husband's text message.

We just got here. Don't start that please. I just want to enjoy my trip. I'm just letting you know that we've made it and are in route to the hotel. I will call you when I get settled into my suite.

-Memori

He responded swiftly.

Make sure you do that. I don't have the time to be worried about you when you shouldn't be gone in the first place, especially not while we going through the shit we going through.

-Nigel

I couldn't formulate a response quick enough. I was going back and forth in my head on how to respond to his reply, but before I was able to, my thoughts were interrupted.

"So, ladies, if you don't mind me asking, is this a pleasure trip for you all or business?" Aquanis asked.

Tiffany and Summer both giggled like schoolgirls before answering the question. They were already sipping on the complimentary champagne found in the fridge of the sprinter.

"Shit, I don't know about these bitches, but I'm trying to have as much fun as I can. So if you're asking me, it's all about the pleasure, baby," Tiffany stated.

All of my friends seemed to be in agreeance as I was face

down into my phone, still attempting to formulate a response to my significant other.

"And what about you, Miss?" Aquanis asked, staring at me from the rearview mirror.

"Whatever they said. I'm no different. I may take care of a little bit of business, but I'm here for my girls to have fun."

"This bitch," I overheard Monica blurt out. It was most certainly the most surprising because she was typically the quiet one in most situations.

"Memori... Memori... Earth to Memori," Tiffany said with one hand over her mouth, snapping her fingers with the other hand to get me to look at her. "Put the phone down for once and enjoy being away from your raggedy ass husband." She removed my phone from my hands and placed it down on my lap. "I know you love him. We all get it, but please don't ruin this trip by letting him affect your mood. You know if you get down, the other girls will get down because they'll be worried about you. We're living real Hakuna Mata-ish this week, or whatever the hell they say on the *Lion King*. Look at me. We leaving that shit where it is for this week, ok? Louisiana is a long ass way away from where we are. He can't hurt you here."

My eye ducts filled, and before I could blink to release a tear, Tiffany had wiped them clean.

"Look, girl, we're going to have a good time, and we will deal with bullshit when it's time to, but right now ain't the time, ok?"

Gathering my composure, she was able to help me get my mind right. I happened to look up in the rearview mirror to fix my makeup and caught the eyes of our tour guide, Aquanis, staring at me. He gave me a gentle head nod to let me know everything would be ok, before he returned his eyes to the road.

The ride from the airport to the hotel resort seemed like it took forever, but once we arrived, it was well worth every moment spent baking in the sprinter.

"Ladies, your oasis awaits," Aquanis uttered, pulling the sprinter to a stop at the entrance of the Four Seasons Hotel.

My girls and I got out of the van and proceeded to the entrance. Aquanis was not too far behind, loading our luggage onto a cart with one of the hotel attendants.

"Welcome to the Four Seasons resort," a hostess stated as we entered the building.

It was beautiful. The floors were marble, and the walls had gold-plated accessories. The pictures we saw when we booked the rooms, did the place absolutely no justice. As we approached the counter to check in, Aquanis walked over to us with both hands behind his back.

"Ladies, once you have gotten your keys, the young gentleman here will have your things taken up to your rooms. Is there anything you need from me before you all go get settled in?"

"No, but thank you," or group echoed one after another.

"You ladies are very welcome. Ah Miss, I left your bag in the sprinter. I know you don't want people touching your things, so I thought that it would be best if I did."

I looked past him at the cart of luggage that was loaded, and he was serious. He really didn't put my shit on there. If looks could kill, I would have shot him right between his eyes.

"You've got to be kidding me. Really?" I questioned.

"Yes, really. Is that a problem for such a strong, independent woman like yourself?" he replied.

Before I could fix my mouth to say anything, he brought both of his hands to the front of him.

"I'm joking, I personally grabbed your things. I hope that's not an issue."

As he smiled, the light shined off his pearl white teeth and danced with the four golden covered fangs. "Would you like for me to put your bag with the rest of the ladies?"

I took a sigh of relief, because I felt myself on the verge of spazzing out on him.

"No, thank you, I've got it. Thank you, Aquanis," I stated reluctantly.

He handed me my bag, and as innocently as he could, rubbed my hand as we made the exchange. I looked up at him, and he gave me that nod yet again. As shady as he looked, there was something about him that made me feel as though things were going to be ok. He had a calming presence to him.

"Ladies, now that you are here, here is my card." He handed each of us his contact card, just in case we needed him outside of his working hours. "If you need anything or would like to go anywhere, don't hesitate to reach out," he emphasized as he handed Tiffany a card. "I know that you all have to get settled in, so I'll leave you all to that."

"Did you see that?" Summer asked, looking towards all of us, noticing the strong gravitational pull he had towards Tiffany.

"You know we saw it, girl," I responded. As he began to walk away, I felt the need to speak up before he got too far away from us. "Aquanis, wait." My girls looked at me, trying to figure out what I was up to. He stopped in his tracks and walked back towards us. "Look, it isn't very often I do this, but I'll admit when I'm wrong. I want to apologize about the way I responded to you at the airport. I'm not used to being catered to, especially not by a man. Nonetheless, I appreciate you doing your job and being polite about it."

He put that beautiful smile of his on display once again and reached out to shake my hand.

"I appreciate the apology, but it's not needed. I'm only here to do my part. I hope that this moment is the way that the rest of our time together on your trip is.

"Ohhhh, bitch, I think somebody like you, not me!" Tiffany exclaimed.

I looked over at my friends and rolled my eyes while trying to hide my smile.

"Is that bitch blushing? You can hide the smile, but them cheeks getting red, girl," Tiffany continued.

"I think your friends are right," Aquanis mentioned with a wink while placing a gentle kiss on my hand before letting it go. "Ladies, enjoy your stay. Please be in touch," he said to the group while waving and walking away. "I will see you all tomorrow morning."

As he made his way out, the concierge clerk gathered our attention.

"Here you are, ladies. Your suites are all on floor number seven. I hope you enjoy your stay with us, and again, welcome to Dubai!"

"Let's get up here, freshen up, and meet up down here around six," Tiffany stated. Everybody cool with that plan? Because a bitch hungry, and I can smell that there is food somewhere close in this resort."

The group agreed, and we went on our way. We were two to a suite, which put me in the same room as Tiffany. Entering the room, Tiffany let out a huge scream.

"Memori, you did this! Do you see this shit? This room is the shit, girl."

The room was a vibe by itself. There were led lights that flowed along the couch and seemed to be playing to the music as we entered.

I allowed Tiffany to choose which room she wanted in the suite before placing my bag in the other room. She screamed again from the room she'd chosen. I sat on the plush, extended King bed and got comfortable. I pulled my phone back out and reread the messages from my husband, preparing to respond now that I was alone. Before I could get the thoughts together to respond to his last message, a barrage of other messages came through now that my iPhone was connected to the Wi-Fi.

So now you just ain't gone respond? I knew you was gone be on that fuck shit when you got around them bald head hoes you hang with.

-Nigel

What kind of shit you on for real right now, Memori? I'm not with this game you attempting to play right now. You better respond asap.

-Nigel

Say less. I sponsor this trip and this the shit you do? You got me all the way fucked up. You gone regret this shit.

-Nigel

I'm in my room finally. I hope that everything is okay at home. I do miss you and apologize about the late response. I have to connect to Wi-Fi over here since you refused to let me upgrade the phone line to the international plan.

-Memori

Good way to deflect that shit on me. I'm going to bed. I'll deal with yo lying ass tomorrow. Tell whatever nigga you with that he can have you for tonight, but you better answer when I call you tomorrow so keep yo ass in that room near the Wi-Fi.

-Nigel

I fell back onto the bed, closing my eyes, trying to ignore the negative in my life. I listened to the music that was coming from the living area of the suite and just tried to get lost in the sounds. That didn't last long as Tiffany barged into my room with her phone going live on Instagram.

"Y'all look at this hoe here, acting like she tired. Memori, get yo' ass up. We about to go turn up."

I threw my hands up and waved to her Instagram following before she walked back out of my room, continuing to entertain her fans. My phone began to vibrate, and I wanted to do nothing more than ignore it, but in doing, so I knew that it would add more fuel to the fire that was burning between my husband and myself. To my surprise, it wasn't my husband; it was my therapist.

Hey, I know that you are on vacation, but wanted to apologize to you about the other day. I know that it wasn't all my fault, but as a patient, you shouldn't be subjected to that kind of behavior from me or anyone else. As far as your visit this week, I want you to know that the option for a virtual visit is on the table for your session if you'd like. If you decide to cancel, please let me know and I will have my assistant remove you from the schedule.

-S.V.

No, I will keep the appointment. I need to get some things off my mind and stay in a good place. Same time as usual is good.

-Memori

Perfect. I will send you a link for the time if that is ok with you and remember that this is a once in a lifetime opportunity. Embrace everything that Dubai has to offer. Don't leave any stone unturned. Enjoy yourself and don't overthink.

- S.V.

My therapist was right. I needed to cut loose and enjoy myself while I was here. The bullshit needed to stay where it was. I got up from the bed and headed into Tiffany's room.

"Hey, girl," I stated, entering her room.

She'd ended her live and was taking pictures on her bed.

"What's up, bestie?" she responded, adjusting her cleavage for her photo.

"Let's go get a drink. I need to relax and get some of this tension off me so that we can have a good time."

Her face lit up. She hadn't heard those words from me in a long time. She sprang up from the bed and came and hugged me.

"That's the Memori I know. Let me change into my bathing suit, and then we can head down. You know the bar is pool side. I'll shoot a text to the other girls to meet us down in the lobby. You know Summer's ass ain't about to turn no liquor down."

Little did I know, that one statement would change the entire outlook of my vacation.

Chapter 6

Sy'Cotic

"Thank you for scheduling the meeting, but I think that we'll be going a different direction," I heard the man on the other end say before disconnecting the call. I took the pen organizer from the desk and tossed it across the room, shattering it. "This shit can't be this hard."

I was due for a much-needed break and decided that I would go down to the bar and blow some steam off. I was attempting to close the deal on the final two properties I needed in the newly renovated section of Dubai. With that rejection, I'd completely struck out, which was unusual for me. I slammed my laptop's screen closed and paced the office portion of my residency apartment. I needed fresh air, liquor, and a different atmosphere, and I knew just where to go. Before I could exit my apartment, I noticed a transaction come through on my phone.

Wire transfer complete.

That was the lone bright spot in my day. I made my way down to the pool side bar. I noticed that the usual weekend rush of tourists had arrived. That was the beauty of Dubai. There was always a cultural melting pot blending in together. I found myself sitting at the bar, taking shot after shot, when I noticed a group of women, all with heavy southern accents that reminded me of home and my mother. They were gathered together, but there was one that caught my eye as she was eyes down, locked into her phone, trailing the group. Three of the four women went to get into the water as that one stayed closer to the land side of the bar. I watched her for a few minutes. She rejected man after man as they approached or offered to buy her a drink. I decided that I would be the oddball and see if I could break the ice with her and at least get a conversation out of her.

As I approached her sitting there, I motioned for the bartender to top her glass off.

"No, thank you," she attempted to say to him, but it was too late. He'd already given her another shot.

"Can you imagine meeting your soul mate after already getting married?" I stated jokingly to her as she sat before me, sipping from her glass of D'ussé with one hand and her phone in the other. I sat with a seat in between us, noticing that she was still engaging in her phone conversation.

"Damn, whoever is on the other end of that paragraph you're typing must've really pissed you off. I'd hate to be the man that reads all of that and has to respond with a thumbs up."

She almost choked on the sip she'd taken as she turned and looked at me with a smirk on her face.

"Excuse me?" she questioned, attempting to keep her laughter contained. "If you must know, it's not a text message. I'm writing a note to myself, Mr. Nosey. Where the hell did you come from anyway?"

"It doesn't matter where I came from. What matters is that I'm here now."

"Oh, really?" she stated.

"Forgive my intrusive nature, however, I noticed the ring and was thinking that I fucked up and allowed another man to marry my soul mate. That shit is crazy," I casually shook my head, looking away from her for a moment before taking a sip of my drink. "As far as me being nosey, it wasn't my intention, I just assumed that you took a vacation away from bullshit and thought that you were at the bar feeding into it. Your facial expressions gave you away, and if I was wrong, my mistake."

"Well, you know what they say about making assumptions," she replied through laughter.

I could tell that she was overtaken by my boldness, but she cracked, and I knew that was my chance to keep the smile there for a while. She placed her phone face down and turned towards me.

"Ahhhhh, there it is. There's the smile. I knew I'd get it out of you. The name is Sy'Cotic, it's a pleasure to meet you," I mentioned, extending my hand to meet hers. She obliged and allowed the formal introduction to take place.

"Sy'Cotic, that's different. Is it a trait or just a name?"

I almost choked on my drink this time, caught off guard by her question.

"That was a good one. As far as it being different, is that in a good way or a bad way?"

"I can't say which way just yet, but it's nice to meet you as well," she responded. "You look just like someone I know. I just can't put my finger on who right now."

The two of us shared a moment as our eyes locked onto one another. In the heat of the stare down, I was deemed the loser as I broke the gaze first, motioning for the bartender to bring another round of our drinks, not too long after her attention was pulled away as one of her friends began yelling at her.

"So, are you going to tell me your name?" I questioned as the two of us played cat and mouse for information. That moment was quickly interrupted by a loud noise coming from the pool area.

"Sincere..." she whispered.

"Sincere, your name is Sincere?"

"No, silly."

"No? Well, again, my name is Sy'Cotic."

"I'm sorry, but you look my therapist. His name is Sincere," she uttered, realizing who it was that I favored and avoiding answering yet another one of my questions.

It was ironic that she would say the name Sincere. I had a brother with that same name, but it had been a long time since I'd heard it. In my eyes, he was dead and never returning. It had to just be a coincidence that there was someone else with the same name that favored me. Her having a therapist and making notes in her phone for herself should have been a red flag to me, yet, I ignored the warning signs. I was intrigued once I saw that she was a smart ass like me; it kept things interesting.

"Aye… Excuse me. Memori, who is this man?"

The woman at the bar with me dropped her head and placed her hand over it.

"Excuse me, sir, who are you?!" one of the woman's friends yelled from the pool with a drink in her hand.

I waved to the group of women and turned back towards the young lady I was entertaining.

"Memori… I like that," I stated, taking a sip of my drink. So should I introduce myself, or are you going to do that for me?"

She waved off her friends and picked her head up, looking at me.

"So, are you a good one or a bad one?" I questioned before taking the remainder of my shot of White Hennessy to the head.

"I wouldn't give you my name. What makes you think I'm about to answer something that ridiculous?"

"Because I've watched you turn away at least ten men in the short amount of time you've been sitting here, and I've managed to keep your attention longer than all of them combined. So, my question remains."

She was once again caught off guard by my question, and once again found herself choking on another sip of drink.

"Damn, are you gone choke every time I ask a question?" I stated with a slight chuckle. I took a napkin from the table and gently reached to wipe the small amount of liquor that managed to escape her lips. She was slightly startled as she jumped back to avoid the contact.

"You got PTSD or something? I ain't gone hurt you. I'm just trying to get the liquor off your lips before it smudges your lipstick."

She relaxed long enough for me to clean the spot, then she began to answer my question.

"You watched me send that many men away, and yet, you decide to bring your ass over here and try to shoot your shot too? Well, it's going to get rejected just like the rest. It's some strange shit for you to notice the number of men that I've sent away. Are you stalking me or something? And what do you mean by, 'am I a good one or a bad one'?"

I laughed lightly at her attempt to deny me.

"Oh, really? If you were going to reject me, I would have been dismissed by now. Am I wrong?" She adjusted her posture and placed both of her hands firmly on the bar island in front of us with her fingers interlocked. "It's exactly as it sounds. Are you a good memory or will you be a bad one?" I questioned with a sardonic smirk.

I could tell by her demeanor that she hadn't met energy like mine, or at least, she hadn't seen it in a while. I wasn't the type to run away or back down when faced with adversity.

"See, that lil' smirk of yours, I can already see what type of shit you on," she responded.

"Chill out," I stated laughing. "I'm just sparking a conversation. Nothing more and nothing less. Besides, I can't go there with you with that rock on your hand. I'm just embracing the opportunity to have a conversation with someone new, that's all."

She cleared her throat as the two of us locked eyes again. I motioned for the bartender once again as she looked down at her ring, twisting it around her finger before allowing words to escape her mouth into the atmosphere again.

"There're thousands of somebody new's in here, and yet, here you are. But if you must know for conversation's sake, it just depends on the situation. For some, I've been an angel. Some others would say I'm a demon. Just like any other human, my traits depend on which me a person is able to bring out."

"Hmmm." I lifted my shot glass, investigating it.

"What's the 'hmmm' for?" she questioned, looking at me with my drink.

I paused for a moment, taking my tongue and circling the top of the glass to remove the salt from its rim. "It's nothing, let's just leave it alone."

"Nah, you've been blunt and Billy Bad Ass this whole time we've been sitting here. Don't let the cat bite your tongue now."

I smiled at her as I looked directly into her eyes.

"To be honest with you, if it wasn't for that ring, I would've loved nothing more but for you to change places with this drink right now. I'd keep the taste of you on my lips for the remainder of the night."

Memori took deep breaths for a short time before she

swallowed her words and turned her head to look away from me.

"Well, it's a good thing that this is for conversation's sake. Whew."

I gave her a smile as her friend came up from the water.

"Excuse me, ma'am, I know you heard me talking to you. You got me coming up, leaving my natural mermaid state to find out what the hell is really going on."

Her friend turned towards me, looking at me from toe to head.

"Hmph."

"How are you today, queen? My name is Sy'Cotic. It's a pleasure to meet you."

I extended my hand to meet hers.

"That's more like it, but good gawd, what's wrong with your voice? You related to God or something? Goodness, sir, I been over here less than a minute, and you've already got me a lil' bit wet. I can only imagine how my girl here is feeling."

"Tiffany!" Memori yelled in shock.

"You might be too much for my little friend right here to handle. She isn't accustomed to all this big di.... masculine energy."

I couldn't help but to laugh as Memori tried her best to quiet her friend.

"Ok, Tiffany, you've met the man, now go back over there with the girls. I'll be over there in a second.

Tiffany took her index and middle finger, pointing them at her eyes then back towards me to signal that she was watching me. I played along with her and raised both of my hands, letting her know that I wasn't going to do any harm to her friend.

Once she got back in the pool, Memori exhaled a sigh of relief.

"I am so sorry about that," she stated.

"It's ok. It no big deal. You have a good friend there. A little animated, but she is a good friend. I can tell that she's good for you. Hang on to her. There aren't too many people out there in the world like that.

She shook her head in agreement.

"Well, I know that you need to get over to your girls, so I'm hopeful that we can finish the conversation before you leave to go back to the states.

"I don't know. I don't think that's a good idea."

"How about this, don't think and just do. I won't take no for an answer. Eight tomorrow evening, if you're free, I'd love to entertain you more and get to know more about you, Memori. If not, I'll be down here, back at the bar, drowning my sorrows.

"If I agree, and only if I decide to take you up on this offer, I will be here. If you don't see me by at least eight fifteen, then you know my answer."

"I'll accept that Memori and hope to see you tomorrow evening."

Chapter 7

Memori

Morning came, and my girls and I were up bright and early to get our day started. We wanted to really embrace the culture in Dubai and see what it had to offer. Tiffany made the arrangements with our tour guide, Aquanis. We decided to grab a bite to eat before we headed out in one of the many dining areas located in the resort.

"Y'all, I'm so ready to get out here and see what this place has to offer. What are we going to do first?" Monica asked.

"I think we should see the big tower thing first. If not that, I think we could always go shopping. You know a bitch stay ready to blow a bag," Summer stated, reaching for her purse.

I remained relatively quiet. There was a lot on my mind that I was going back and forth on. Not to mention the fact that I'd spent most of the night going back and forth with Nigel over FaceTime.

"Fuck where we're going. We need to have a talk with and about Miss Thang over here," Tiffany stated looking in my direction.

"Who? Me? What the hell I do?" I questioned, confused.

"What I do? Don't act brand new. Last night while we were all in the pool, enjoying the water, yo' ass was up here exchanging words with that dark piece of fine ass meat. What was that about?"

"It was nothing. I was just passing time. Nothing more, nothing less."

"Passing time my ass, bitch. I haven't seen you give us the amount of time you gave that man last night, and that genuine smile you had on your face let me know that he was saying some shit that kept you on your toes."

"I wonder what the mister would say," Monica responded.

Tiffany and I both cut our eyes in her direction, and my lip flared up at her.

"It was nothing, seriously," I replied.

Just as they began riding my ass about Sy'Cotic, he walked by the restaurant that we were eating in, dressed in a suit. I guess they noticed him as well because they all looked at me at once.

"Do you see what I see?" Monica stated, watching him from a distance.

"Uh huh," the group echoed like a choreographed scene in a movie.

Tiffany was the first to snap back to reality.

"Speak of the devil and he shall appear. You gone walk over there and finish your conversation?"

I shook my head no and sipped from the glass of Mimosa in front of me.

"Bitch, you can't hide them rosie red cheeks right now. He must have said some good shit to you. Y'all see this shit? Memori done got out here to Dubai and decided that she was gone show her ass. Let me find out all that arguing you and ole boy was doing was fake. I'ma whoop yo' ass," Tiffany continued on as I tuned her out.

Sy'Cotic walked past the restaurant once more; this time,

with his head face first in a newspaper, sipping his beverage from Starbucks.

"Thank goodness he didn't see us," I uttered, holding my breath in, trying to make myself invisible. Although he was looking rather dapper in his attire and almost had a glide to his stride as he walked, I didn't want to be bothered. It did spark my curiosity watching him, however. I must have completely zoned out thinking because Tiffany was snapping her fingers, attempting to get me back to reality.

"Damn, Memori, what did he say to you for real, girl? You literally just spent sixty seconds of your life watching this man's movement."

"He didn't say anything; let's just let it go."

They all looked at me with snarled lips but ultimately changed the subject. Although several shots were thrown my way during breakfast, I stood my ground and didn't reveal anything that was said.

"Ladies, your chariot awaits you," Aquanis stated, walking over to us. His timing was impeccable.

"Right on time, my man," I stated, pouncing up from my seat, giving him a high five.

"Oh yeah, there's definitely some shit going on with this girl. We gone find out what it is."

Speed walking ahead of the pack, I tried to rush to the sprinter van. I sent a text to Nigel to inform him that I'd be unavailable while I was out. In my rushing, I bumped into a gentleman, standing right outside the door. He dropped his things, and my phone went flying.

"Shit, I am so sorry, sir," I stated with concern in my voice.

He turned around slightly upset, but that quickly changed once he saw me. Of all the men to bump into, it had to be Sy'Cotic.

"Well, good morning, Memori. If you wanted my attention, all you had to do was say good morning."

"I…"

"Well, well, well. Now I know why she was walking so fast. Good morning, mister man.

He smiled at my friends and spoke candidly.

"Ladies, good morning. He dropped to his knees to retrieve both his newspaper and my phone. "Are we good? And are you ok?" he asked, placing my cracked phone into my hands.

"No, no no no no," I whimpered, looking down at my phone.

"Look, I got you," he said gently. "Aquanis, come here."

Aquanis was busy helping Tiffany get into the sprinter when he heard Sy'Cotic call him. He rushed over to us and was given specific instructions.

"So, do you two know each other?" I questioned, standing next to the van.

Sy'Cotic looked at me and smirked. He pointed to the sprinter van. The side of it had *SY'CO.* printed on the side.

"Yeah, you can say we know each other. He actually works for me."

I was impressed. He took my phone from my hands and gave it to Aquanis.

"Aquanis will get your phone fixed while you guys are out today. You should be back up and running by the end of the night.

"Thank you. I appreciate that," I responded, overwhelmed with gratitude.

"Besides, I need you to be able to tell what time it is so you're not late tonight," he stated, laughing.

I turned to look at my girls to make sure that none of them heard him.

"I haven't made you any guarantees or promises yet, but as of now, we're still on. Remember eight fifteen is my rule."

I headed over to the entrance of the sprinter and got in. Silence filled the sprinter as all attention was on me. As soon as the door closed, you would have thought that we were on a game show the way the girls began to ask me questions.

"OK, Memori, for real girl, what's going on?" Tiffany asked.

"It is seriously nothing. He invited me to dinner tonight. I haven't made any decisions, but I have thought about it."

"Girl, do you see that man? What is there to think about?" Summer asked, twerking in her seat.

"She is still married, dumb ass girl. We can't just sell her off to the highest bidder," Monica stated.

"Married or not, her husband halfway around the world, and hell, they don't like each other half the time anyway," Summer replied.

I just looked at her with fire in my eyes, trying not to get upset.

"Ladies, we're not about to do that right here, not right now," Tiffany responded, coming to my aid. "Memori, I'm all for you having fun. Enjoy yourself; you're on vacation, but be careful. As good as he looks, men like that can be trouble, just think about what you're doing. I don't want you any more hurt that you need to be.

As usual, Tiffany was right. I was still a married woman, and I shouldn't have even be entertaining the thoughts of another man. I put Sy'Cotic in the back of my mind as we began to drive deeper into the city.

"Ladies, welcome to our first stop. This is one of the tallest buildings in the world, if not the tallest. Welcome to the Burj Khalifa," Aquanis stated as we parked in the parking lot across from the building.

As we stepped out of out of the van, we all looked up in awe. Again, it was one of those situations where the pictures did no justice to the actual site once you witnessed it. It felt like we were looking up into a never-ending sky.

"Please ladies, follow me," he instructed.

We entered the building, and there were people everywhere. It was arguably the biggest attraction that Dubai had to offer mainstream. We walked over to get into the line as Aquanis went to talk to one of the workers towards the front of the line. A few moments later, he came back over to us with four passes and a smile on his face.

"Ladies, I'm pleased to tell you that the owner of our company made arrangements for you all to skip the line and take the express pass up to the top. Now we will have to find something else to compliment your day in place of the time you would have spent waiting in line, but this is gonna save you a couple hours of waiting.

The girls and I all looked at each other. Without hesitation, we jumped out of the public line and went over to the express line.

"And y'all still don't think that she should give this man any play?" Summer questioned.

"He's definitely trying to grab her attention; that's a fact," Monica replied.

As we ascended to the top of the tower, the kind act definitely didn't go unnoticed in my mind. The fact that this man owned his own business in Dubai was intriguing enough to put a little more thought into having the dinner date with him. It wasn't every day that you saw a black, successful man in America, let alone another country.

The elevator dinged on the top floor, and we stepped off. You could literally see everything that Dubai had to offer. It was beautiful. No, it was amazing. Like most of the tourists there, my girls pulled their phones out and snapped a few pictures to remember the attraction.

"Do you mind if I take a picture with you ladies?" Aquanis asked.

None of us seemed to have a problem with it as we motioned him over, allowing him into the photo shoot. Tiffany, being who she was, wrapped her arms around his waist as he held his phone up into the sky to get the aerial view of all us and the background at the same time.

"If you hold on to me like this, you may not be going back to the states," he said jokingly.

Tiffany took both of her hands and slid them down the front of his torso towards his belt buckle.

"If you play your cards right, I may not — seriously."

She'd stood right in the middle of the Burj Khalifa and groped this man's penis. The echo of 'ooh' sounded off as the girls and I noticed the blatant flirting between the two of them.

We broke apart from taking pictures as a group. Tiffany had taken Aquanis's phone and started taking several selfies of the two of them. It didn't seem like I was the only one having male attention here in Dubai. After a couple hours inside the tower, we made our way back to the sprinter and on to our next destination.

As we approached the next stop, we noticed that the building was massive. Aquanis gave its introduction and made sure to let us know where we were.

"I hope you ladies brought enough money. There isn't a store you can think of that isn't located in here. Welcome to the Dubai mall."

Summer was the first out of the van and probably the most excited about this portion of the trip. The rest of us exited the van and began to prepare for our shopping journey.

"Hey, Mrs. Memori, there's a facility in here that I can have your phone fixed. I'm just letting you know I'll break away from you guys at some point to go handle that for you."

"Thank you for that, Aquanis, I truly appreciate it. You can tell your boss I said thank you as well."

Aquanis led the way, escorting us into the building. The word massive was an understatement. It truly didn't describe how big this place really was. He was correct. Every single store that you could think of was in here. Every designer brand that you could think of was housed in this one building.

"Well girls, where should we begin?" Summer questioned like a kid in a candy shop.

"Girl, you know we're following you. Didn't nobody bring that much money with them. None of us have old, rich, white ex-husbands," Tiffany said jokingly.

Summer chuckled but led us right into the Louis Vuitton store.

We began to look around the store, and I fell in love with a pair of gorgeous heels. I reached into my purse, wanting to check my account balance, only to realize that I didn't have my phone, and even if I did, I wasn't going to be able to check the balance without Wi-Fi. I walked over to Summer, who was checking out the handbags in the store.

"Hey girl, can I see your phone really quick? I need to make a call."

She reached into her purse and handed me her phone. Be

quick, girl, and don't be going through my pictures. You might see something you aren't supposed to. The both of us laughed for a second, and I proceeded to handle my business.

I called the number on the back of my card, attempting to get my balance, however, it was requiring a security code that I had forgotten.

"Shit," I thought out loud.

The only other person that had that code was Nigel, but I didn't want to call him because it was roughly one in the morning back home. Then again, he usually stayed up late anyway, so I thought to myself, *what the fuck?* and gave it a try. The phone rang a couple times before he answered.

"I've been waiting on your call," he answered in a low tone.

"Uh hello?" I responded.

"What's up?"

I looked at the phone, confused for a second.

"Nigel, whose call were you waiting on?"

"Memori," he sounded perplexed, not expecting me to be on the other end of the phone.

"Don't fucking play with me. Who did you think it was, and whose call are you waiting on this late at night?"

I was starting to get loud and make a scene in the store as other patrons began to look at me.

"I wasn't waiting on anybody call. I was just talking out loud. What's up, and where is your phone? Why are you calling me from somebody else's number?"

"I'm using one of the girls' phones because mine is broken. It slipped out of my hand earlier, and the screen cracked, but it's being repaired. I need to know if you remember the passcode that we set up to my account. I'm trying to check my balance because I'd like to make a purchase while I'm over here.

"I don't remember the passcode, but I can log in on my phone and check to see what the balance is. What the hell are you trying to buy anyway? It's not like you need anything else.

We couldn't get through one conversation without it being some drama.

"That doesn't matter. It's just a pair of shoes that I saw. Can you log in and let me know real quick, please?

He got quiet, as if he was backing away from the phone to do as I'd asked for a second.

"You got a closet full of shoes that you already don't wear. Why the hell are you gonna buy some more shoes? That makes no fucking sense." He took a deep breath, and I could tell that he was frustrated. "Hold the fuck on, let me check this balance so you can get the hell off my phone. You do realize it's nighttime over here, right?"

"I do realize that, and I apologize for calling so late, but we're out and about. I'm at the mall, and I don't have access to my information. If you get a chance later in the day, will you please activate the international plan on my phone?"

"Memori, we've had this discussion, and I already told you that I'm not adding that shit to the plan. Why would I make the bill go up for you to be gone for just a week? That makes no fucking sense. If push comes to shove, you can call me, just like you're calling me right now from one of your girls' phones or wait till yo' ass is connected to some Wi-Fi."

"That's fine, but you don't have to catch an attitude with me. I'm just trying to make this as simple as possible for the both of us.

"If you wanted to make this shit simple for both of us, you would have kept your ass at home."

"I really don't want to argue with you right now, Nigel. Can you please just give me my balance so I can go ahead about my day?"

"Wait a fuckin' minute." He paused, and his breathing pattern changed. Where the fuck did all this money come from, Memori? It's showing here that you got fourteen thousand in checking and another twenty-seven thousand in savings."

I really wished I didn't have to call him to get that balance, however, I needed to know. It wasn't like he didn't already have access to see those numbers; he just never took advantage of what he had.

"I've been saving my money. I have no reason to blow it frivolously. Granted, I have a bunch of items. I usually shop on a budget, and I rarely splurge on myself, so I'm able to just save my money."

"Uh huh. Well, when you get back, we're going to look over these bills and make sure you're able to splurge on some of them. You good now that you've got what you called for? Is there anything else that you need right now? I'm about to try to take my ass to bed, I gotta get up and go to work in the morning."

"No, but I love you and thank you."

"Uh-huh. We will talk later, goodnight."

He disconnected the line, and I walked back over by the handbags and handed Summer her phone back.

"Thanks, girl. I appreciate you," I stated as the phone began to vibrate.

I tried to quickly look at the number, just in case it was Nigel texting me that he loved me since he didn't verbalize it. The number looked like his, but she quickly opened the text and replied to it.

"Anytime, girl. You know I got you."

"Hey, if the number I just called texts you, let me know. I had to call Nigel from your phone to get some information."

Her eyes got wide for second, but she agreed. I walked back over to the heels section as she continued her shopping for bags and picked out a couple pair of heels that I thought would be cute for me.

"Oh, so my bitch buying heels and shit now. I hope this ain't for that 'not a date' that you got later."

"Come on, Tiffany. Now you know me better than that. Besides, I haven't guaranteed that I would even go with the guy."

"You're right. I do know you better than that, and that's why I'm going out on a limb and telling you to not listen to yourself right now. The last time you bought a pair of heels for yourself was when you and lil' dude had just started dating. So, you can say what you want to, but all signs look like you've already made up in your mind that you're going on this date.

I had no come back. I had no response. I just turned back towards the heels and continued shopping. It was very impulsive of me, but in my mind, I was just doing something for myself for once.

Several hours passed, and the girls and I had finally made our way back to the resort with all the bags that we'd bought.

"I am tired, girl, do you hear me?" Tiffany stated as we got into our room. She tossed all her bags onto the floor and flopped down on the couch in the living area of the suite.

"Tired is an understatement. I'm right there with you. I think I'm gonna go lay down for a second before we do anything else."

"Do your thang, best friend. I might just take a nap right here where I'm at. I can't walk another step."

I got into my bedroom, put my belongings down, and began to go through my purse, looking for my phone.

"Shit."

In the madness of the day with all the shopping, I failed to get my phone back from Aquanis. I walked back into the living room, attempting to use Tiffany's phone, but my girl really was worn out. She was already asleep. I really didn't have an urgent need for my phone; it was just for convenience. Nigel was at home asleep, so I really didn't have to worry about hearing from him, and all of the girls that I typically talked to were here with me. I went back inside the room, stretched out on the bed, and took a nap.

Some time passed, and I was less than an hour away from my decision on if I was going to meet Sy'Cotic.

There's no harm in dinner and conversation. I thought aloud to myself as I began to go through my wardrobe, trying to figure out what to wear. After seeing both sides of his attire, I didn't want to be overly dressed, but I didn't want to be underdressed either. Ultimately, finding something to wear was going to be the deciding factor on if I would go or not.

"Tiffany, come here real quick, please."

Tiffany walked into the room and noticed the clothes spread out across the bed.

"So, we're doing this?" she questioned rather excited. "Are you really going?

"If you think it's a bad idea, I won't."

"Does my face say that this is a bad decision? I can't make that decision for you, but like I told you, if you do go through with it, just be careful."

She looked down at the clothes and how I had them aligned and began to mix and match different sequences.

"If it were me and I was going to go, I wouldn't want to be too revealing, but I'd want to tease him enough to make him think that I'm interested. With that being said, I would go with this dress and the new heels, just to give him a teaser of the bad bitch you really are.

Tiffany always had a way with style, and seeing her vision before me, I understood her point of view.

"Go ahead and get ready, girl, because it looks like you're going."

She helped ease my mind, and it was finally made up. I was at least going to give him an opportunity for conversation. As for myself, I just wanted to step outside of my normal and live a little bit.

"Hey girl, can you do me a favor while I'm in the shower getting ready? Will you reach out to Aquanis and figure out what the deal with my phone is? I didn't get it back before we left the mall and completely forgot until we got back up here.

"I got you, girl. Now go get ready before you change your mind."

Chapter 8

Sy'Cotic

Eight o'clock rolled around, and I hadn't seen any signs of her yet. She did give me the inclination that she wouldn't show until a bit later, and the time she mentioned hadn't hit quite yet, so I gave her the benefit of the doubt. I sat by the poolside bar just as I did the night before, waiting to see if she was going to show up. Regardless of if she did or didn't, I knew I had a way to get to her. She'd forgotten to retrieve her phone from Aquanis, and he brought it to me once they returned from their outing. One way or another, I knew I'd be able to at least see her once more.

Her phone was connected to the hotel's Wi-Fi, and it consistently buzzed in my pocket. Each time it did, I made sure to silence it. I ordered a drink as I continued to sit and wait for her to make her appearance. Both anxious and nervous, I remained in place as the clock ticked closer to eight fifteen.

The time rolled past just as the clock kept moving. So, eight twenty as well as eight twenty-five. I had my answer, and that was enough for me to pay for my drink at the bar and head back up to my residency apartment. Just as I began to do exactly that, I heard a very sweet, faint voice behind me.

"Damn, you're leaving already?"

I turned around, slowly looking and before my eyes, there Memori stood. She looked truly amazing. Her dress wasn't too tight, yet it wasn't too loose. It showed just enough of her curves to make a man wanna continue glancing at her.

"Wow, you look amazing. Late, but you look amazing."

"Better late than never. Just be glad I even showed up," she replied.

I started at her feet and worked my eyes up to the top of head.

"I'm damn sure glad that you decided to."

"Well, it's to be determined if I'm glad that I decided to, but you have the opportunity to tilt the scale with me being here."

Before I could speak another word, I felt my pocket vibrating. I reached in for my phone but noticed that it wasn't mine going off. I looked at the caller ID and noticed the initials S.V.

Memori looked at me, waiting for me to make a move towards whatever restaurant we were going to eat at. While doing so, she noticed the phone that I'd just pulled out of my pocket.

"That's a pretty pink case you have there."

"HA! You're funny. You know damn well I wouldn't have a pink case."

I handed her the phone as the vibrations were coming to an end.

"Is that my phone? Wait, why do you have my phone?"

"Aquanis failed to give it to you when you guys got back earlier, and he had to rush off to get to some things that he had to handle. He told me he left it in the sprinter, so I went and retrieved it. I figured that I would see you this evening, and if I didn't, my plan was to call you girls and hold your phone for ransom.

She just glared at me with no real emotion on her face.

"That is some fucked up, twisted shit," she stated. "So, had I decided to not show up, you were just gonna keep my phone and make me see you?"

I shook my head yes. "Pretty much. One way or another, I

needed your attention."

"And why is that?"

"Well, I can't get to know you if I can't have a conversation with you."

She shook her head and conceded defeat on this rather small debate.

That was clever on your end; I'll give you that. Although, I feel like you might have told Aquanis not to give me my phone on purpose just for that reason.

I gave her a smirk and a slight wink. "If only I had been smart enough to actually do that, I would take credit for it, but unfortunately, he seriously made a mistake and didn't hand it to you when you guys got out the car."

She peeked down at the phone at all the missed notifications then back up at me.

"Well, I appreciate your honesty and you giving me my phone back but ummm... I'm hungry, so where are we going to eat?"

I dropped my head after giving her a smile and slightly bent my arm for her to interlock hers with mine.

"We have reservations in the dining district here at the resort. We're going to the Mercury Lounge."

I didn't want to go to fancy, yet I didn't want her to feel like she was going to be eating fast food either. The Mercury was a rooftop dining area with a vibe to it. There was a live DJ nightly, and it was just a nice place to relax and enjoy the evening. As we approached the rooftop's entrance, her phone began to buzz again.

"Oh no, I completely forgot. I really need to take this quickly. Give me one moment."

She answered the FaceTime call from the S.V. contact.

"Hey, I am so sorry, doc, I completely lost track of time. Is there any way we could reschedule?"

"Of course, Memori," I heard the man state as I eavesdropped on their conversation.

"Thank you! Thank you so much," she said empathetically.

"We can set the appointment up whenever it's convenient for you. Are you enjoying your trip thus far and is everything ok?"

She looked in my direction then back towards the phone before nodding her head towards the screen.

"So far so good. I haven't had any episodes and have been doing really well managing my emotions."

"Good! Well, I look forward to hearing all about your experiences soon. Please be sure to reach out to Shianne and schedule that appointment. Until then, pran swen bèl!"

I cut my eyes towards her phone as the call came to an end. Pran swen bèl was terminology I hadn't heard since I was a boy. It was quite perplexing to hear it from who I assumed was her therapist. Nevertheless, the time for that conversation would come.

Up-tempo music played as we walked through the entrance and found ourselves a table. The two of us were seated and allowed the conversation to form.

"I take it that was your therapist?"

"Damn, you nosey, but if you must know, yes, it was."

"Pran swen bèl. That's a little close to crossing a line with him, calling you beautiful, isn't it? He's Haitian, right?"

She paused for a second and looked at me.

"Yeah, he is. Wait, how'd you know what that statement meant?"

I gave her a wink and changed the subject.

"That's irrelevant. What matters is right here, right now."

She fixed her posture and had her lips prepared to speak, but the waitress came to the table to get our drink order.

"Can I start you all off with the house wine today, Mr. Baptiste?" the waitress asked."

I took my hands and pointed to Memori, deflecting the drink selection over to her.

"The house wine will be just fine."

As the waitress headed towards the wine cellar, Memori began to dig into who I was.

"Mr. Baptiste, huh? So that's how you know what that statement means. She paused for a second then came back around to my name, Sy'Cotic Baptiste. So, tell me, how does one with a Haitian Creole name end up in Dubai?"

"It's a rather long story. And I don't feel like this is the appropriate setting dig into it, if you will. I will say this, business opportunities drew me here when I was younger. Ever since then, I've found Dubai to be a home away from home."

She just stared at me.

"What's wrong? Was my answer not sufficient?" I asked, looking back at her.

"Nothing, it's just the resemblance between you and my therapist is striking. It's like you guys could seriously be brothers. It's so crazy. So, since you couldn't give me the full story on how you got here, I know that you didn't originate here. Tell me, where are you from?"

"You just gone dig into it anyway, huh? I was originally born in Florida, South Florida to be exact. Down in Little Haiti.

Then, when I was about nine years old, my family moved to Louisiana."

She threw up an L with her hand. It was a typical sign with people from the boot.

"Hey, that's one thing we got in common. I was born and bred in Louisiana."

"I could tell. Your accent was one of the things that attracted me to you when you all first got here. Listening to you all speak gave me a sense of home. I don't get that too often being out here."

She gave me a smile as the waitress approached us with our drinks.

"So outside of owning your business, what else do you do? Dubai is huge, but considering that you stay here, you've had to do everything that you could possibly do. Do you ever get bored and miss home?"

I cleared my throat before I answered. The thought of home was troublesome to me, and I was so busy drowning myself in work and making sure that my businesses were successful, I never took the time to really smell the roses here.

"I really don't know. I don't go out much, and if I do, it's typically down to the bar then I'm back up to my place to work. There're only so many times you can go to the top of the Burj Khalifa and enjoy it. Eventually, you'll develop a sense of vertigo."

"That sounds like a boring life," she replied.

"I wouldn't say that it's boring; I just keep myself grounded in my work. That way, I don't get in trouble. The laws out here are different and a lot stricter. The last thing I want to do is cause any trouble. I've had enough of that in my lifetime.

"What does that mean?" she questioned.

"That means that we're not gonna dig into that at this table right now. We're gonna enjoy the evening and leave old wounds closed.

Just as I made the statement, her phone began to buzz. She looked down at the caller ID, and I could see the shift in her attitude. She exhaled a deep sigh of frustration while reading whatever message came through.

"Everything OK?" I questioned.

She hesitated then shook her head to fix her attitude.

"Yes, everything is fine. I'm not going to let this ruin our conversation. It's just my husband.

"Hmmm."

"Hmmm what?"

"I'm just looking at your demeanor, and I can tell that there's a lot more behind that statement. Your husband shouldn't make you feel the way you're feeling right now, so how about we do this?"

I placed my phone on the table, placing it on do not disturb and motioned for her to do the same. Rather reluctant initially, she did the same.

"I want to be able to give you my undivided attention, and I don't want him to alter your mood. I enjoy seeing the room light up when you smile, so I need you to keep one on your face."

Right on cue, she smiled. Her eyes slightly squinted when she did, and I liked that about her.

"I'm sure you hear this all the time, but you are truly beautiful."

Her smile widened as she began to blush.

"Now how you gonna say something about my therapist

calling me beautiful, and you gone sit here and do the same thing? That's not very professional."

The two of us shared a laugh.

"The difference is, I don't know your secrets, he does. Besides, you're paying him. This is all on me, unless you plan on footing this bill.

She shook her head no, and we shared yet another small laugh. Our food made its way to the table, and the two of shared small talk, just enjoying the company of one another. Once again, her phone began to buzz. This time, it was one of her girls, and she was obligated to answer.

"Hey girl….. Yes, I'm fine…. Don't worry, he's behaving," she stated, looking over at me. "We will be done soon…. I got you, girl. Bye, Tiff."

"I am so sorry about that," she stated as her attention returned to me. "She was worried and had to call more than once, obviously to get through. I didn't want her stressed out."

"No worries, that's what good friends are for."

Concluding our meal, the DJ began playing a song that she took a liking to as she began dancing in her seat. Standing to my feet, I took my hand and extended it to take hers into it. Neither of us knew the lyrics, yet the beat had resemblances of home. It felt like we were back on the second line. She was in her element with the music as she continued enjoying the rhythm and so was I, dancing with her. As the song came to an end, I pulled her in close to me, holding her in my arms with a smile. She looked up at me and embraced the hug before pushing herself away and adjusting her hair.

"Ummm…." she uttered. "Thank you for the dance, but I think we should get ready to go. My girls are worried about me."

I adjusted my shirt and shook my head in agreeance.

Knowing that she was still married, my actions made the moment awkward, and I didn't want her uncomfortable. I walked over to the table and grabbed our belongings after leaving money for our food and a tip. She waited for me by the door as the two of us headed back towards the residence side of the resort.

"I truly appreciate you taking me up on my offer. I enjoyed your company."

She looked down at her phone after removing the do not disturb feature, and it seemed like a never-ending vibration pattern took over as we entered the elevator to her floor.

"Fuckkkkk," she mumbled, looking at a photo and a long message from someone. "Look, I'm glad you invited me. You've been nothing but a gentleman. I appreciate that. I needed that, but the reality is, I can't allow myself to go there and get sucked into a fairy tale that we both know won't happen. So again, thank you for dinner, the conversation, the dance, but I know me, and I don't want to hurt myself or you."

"I respect the honesty, I truly do, but allow me the opportunity to continue getting to know you, at least on a friendly level for the remainder of time that you're here."

"But why? Nothing is going to come from it."

"Why not?"

Her phone began to buzz again. From her face, I could already tell who it was. The elevator came to a halt, and we started towards her suite's door. She reached in for a hug, and she kissed my cheek.

"Thank you, but look, I really must go take care of this. Thank you again, and I'm pretty sure I'll see you around."

She went into her room, answering the phone before the door closed in my face. Little did she know, her playing hard to get was adding fuel to my fire. She wasn't going to get rid of me that easily.

Chapter 9

Memori

Morning came and I was up bright and early. The events from the night before both entertained and troubled me. It let me know that I was in way over my head, playing with fire. I needed to blow off some steam. I hadn't had a workout since we touched down in Dubai, and I felt bothered by that. I was in dire need to not only burn some calories but to also relieve some stress.

Tiffany was still sleep, so I decided to head down by myself. I got down to the gym and noticed that there was an overwhelming amount of testosterone in the building. Nonetheless, I was there simply to get my work out on. I walked by all the cable weight machines and began jogging on the treadmill.

The view was amazing. There were these giant windows that overlooked the beach down below.

No sooner than I got into a rhythm running, the treadmills beside me both got filled with men attempting to get my attention. One of them looked like one of the men I'd already rejected down by the bar my first day here. The other was completely out of my league and nowhere near my type. They both began fighting for my attention, waving their hands, but I continued looking down towards the beach below, jogging on the treadmill with my AirPods in. They eventually figured out that I was uninterested and both left.

I spent about ten minutes on the treadmill, getting a good sweat going before heading over to the stair climber. Once there,

I was able to see the entire gym and everyone in it. That was when I noticed a man in a hoodie lifting dumbbells, grunting as he rotated his arms. I couldn't get a good glimpse of his face with the hoodie over his head, but from the back, he looked like he was chiseled from stone. The back of his arms was defined and solid. He looked up into the mirror and noticed me watching him workout.

"Oh no, please don't see me. Please don't see me," I whispered out loud to myself.

He did happen to see me. It was Sy'Cotic. He readjusted his posture while nodding in the mirror and got back to his lifting. I knew that it would be a matter of time before he came over and spoke to me. Until he did, I was going to focus on my work out and do what I came to do.

An hour passed, and I'd completed my workout. I noticed that Sy'Cotic was still in the building and hadn't come to speak, which was rather odd. I took it upon myself to go speak to him. As I approached, I noticed that he had his Beats by Dre headphones on. I tapped his shoulder as he rested in between his reps on the leg press. He looked up at me and raised his eyebrow.

"What's up, Memori?" he asked dryly, releasing the stopper to complete another rep.

"I just wanted to come speak. I thought it would be rude to be in the same room and not speak. Are you ok?"

"I'm good, I appreciate you for asking," he responded, exerting his energy into the machine.

"Well, I'll let you get back to it. I don't want to interrupt you anymore."

I walked away from him, putting a little extra in my walk, hoping that it would capture his attention, but it was to no avail, which gave me some slight concerns that I'd upset him with the way we parted. He was completely different than he was the night before. I tried to put it in the back of my mind, but I was for certain that the way things went the night before had everything to do with the way he was coming off.

As I got back up to the seventh floor, I could hear music blasting. I opened the door to my suite, and of course, it was coming from my room. As I entered, I noticed a massive bouquet of red and white roses. A card was attached with my name on it.

Not all fairy tales are meant to last forever. Some only last if you allow them.

-Sy

Tiffany came out of the bathroom in a towel, singing at the top of her lungs. I must have startled her as she let out a scream, raising her hands, allowing the towel to fall to the floor.

"Memori, I thought you were gone with ole boy again. I didn't think you'd be back already."

"Nah, I thought I'd nip that situation in the bud.

"Apparently not," she responded, picking up her towel, looking at the roses. Her room door opened, and a head popped out.

"You ok?" a man's voice stated, trying to see what was going on.

Her eyes got wide as she rushed over to the door.

"Tiffany!" I exclaimed, looking at her.

"Look bitch, I don't have in-house dick at home, and I only have one life to live. I'm about to live it up."

I wasn't mad at my girl. To know Tiffany was to love Tiffany, and she lived with absolutely no regrets.

"Is that Aquanis?" I asked.

"Yeah, it's me," he stated from the other room.

She palmed her face and shook her head.

"This ain't us being discreet, man. Shut yo' ass up and get ready." She returned her words towards me as she adjusted her towel. "Look girl, I love you, but I got some shit to handle. This nigga thinks he can make me tap out, so I'm about to make him eat my ass like a rack of ribs."

The two of us laughed and gave each other a high five.

"Handle your business, sis. Make sure that you wrap it up."

"You already know, girl." She entered her room, and I prepared for a shower myself. I was in dire need of one after my workout.

The faint scent of Sy'Cotic's cologne hit my nose. It was as if he sprayed it on the card himself before the card got to me. I read the card once again, just thinking about the words. The gesture was heartwarming. I couldn't think of the last time that I'd received a rose. How he'd managed to pull that off while working out was beyond me, but I was grateful. For his demeanor to be what it was in the gym, this was a sincerely fine gesture.

After my shower, I headed into my room and stretched out on the bed. I overheard Tiffany and Aquanis in an all-out wrestling match. Between her screaming and his moaning, I didn't know what to think. I put my AirPods in my ear and began scrolling through my Instagram feed. There were several pictures I was tagged in, and I noticed Nigel placing the heart emojis under some of them. It warmed my heart to think he was starting to get some act right and missed me.

Hey, I hope your day is going well. Was thinking of you.

-Memori

It was almost two hours later before he responded.

Miss you too you good?

-Nigel

Finally, and yes I am good. I noticed the hearts on Instagram and thought I'd stop being a bitch and try to make things right.

-Memori

Instagram??? I haven't liked shit of yours on Instagram. You must be mistaking me for that therapist nigga or something. What are you talking about? I'm glad you're finally realizing you were wrong tho. About damn time.

-Nigel

I put my phone down and collected my thoughts. I went back to the Instagram feed and took a screenshot of one of his emojis beneath the picture I was tagged in. Before I responded with the picture, I reread the message and quickly realized that he was still on the same little boy shit he'd been on. I proceeded to send him the picture then followed up with an additional text.

I thought that we could talk like adults, but on second thought, I'll let you enjoy your day.

-Memori

He replied with the peace emoji, and although it shouldn't have, it got under my skin. The audacity of him was beyond me. I kept telling myself not to stoop to his level. I tried everything in my power to keep a level head and ignore the thoughts brewing, but it was hard and the shit was weighing heavy on me.

Chapter 10

Sy'Cotic

"Hey, boss." I'm a little under the weather. Do you think that you could find someone to cover for me?" Aquanis stated.

"Shit, you're putting me in a tight place. Is there any way you can try to come in?

The sound of vomit hitting the toilet echoed in his background. "On second thought, take the day. I'll cover you. Text me the info you have for whatever the plan was for today. I'll personally cover."

"Sending it now," he responded through painful breathing.

The call disconnected, and I sat back in my chair, putting away my current day's work. I took a deep breath and waited for the message to come.

Once received, I reviewed the itinerary on the picture message. I was impressed with the list that Aquanis managed to create for the ladies' outing today. I looked down at my attire and realized that I was far too overdressed for the day and decided to put on my uniform from when I first started the company as a one man show. It was a little snug, but I would get the job done. I went down to the truck to do the daily inspection because I didn't want anything to go wrong. I held myself to the same standard that I held my drivers. Not too much time passed, and I found myself parked outside the resort, waiting for the ladies.

The group came down, and to their surprise, it was me and

not Aquanis standing by the truck.

"Uhhh, what are you doing here?" Memori questioned, seeing me positioned next to the vehicle.

"I'll be your driver today. Aquanis is sick."

Her eyes got wide as she turned and looked back at her friend.

"What's wrong?" I questioned, noticing the change in demeanor.

"Nothing, nothing at all. Well sir, are you going to get the door for us?"

They'd managed to catch me off guard and rusty on the job. I opened the door and allowed the ladies in. Moments later, we were off.

"I hope that you ladies are prepared for the day ahead. It's going to be filled with some of the best attractions Dubai has to offer." As we arrived in the middle of the desert sand, the ladies looked at one another and began to talk amongst themselves.

"Aye man, I know damn well you didn't bring us all the way out here to kill us. If we need to sacrifice Memori, then so be it," Tiffany stated. "Memori, give that man a little bit of pussy. We too young to die."

I began to laugh as hard as I could as I looked into the rearview mirror, noticing the terror that was truly in their faces.

"Please relax. I'm not here to kill anyone, unless they fuck with you all," I replied, looking in the rearview mirror at Memori.

"Then what the hell are we doing here?" Monica questioned.

Just as I was about to answer, the ATVs began coming over the hill.

"That's why you're here. Have you all ever had the

opportunity to drive an ATV?"

The energy in the sprinter quickly changed from nervousness to excitement.

"Hell fucking yeah. Let's go," Tiffany stated as she was the first to jump out of the sprinter and run towards them.

Each lady had an ATV and listened to the instructions coming from the instructor.

"We will go over this hill. Down to the next station, we have a surprise set up for you ladies. Did you all bring your bags with your change of clothes? I don't see any with you."

All of them looked around at each other as I tried to creep back into the sprinter.

"We didn't know we needed a change of clothes," one of them spat. Before I knew it, Memori walked over to me, shaking her head.

"You know Aquanis would have had us prepared. You should be ashamed of yourself," she mentioned jokingly.

"No worries. If you don't have clothing with you, we have a station where you can change and a dressing room," the instructor mentioned.

"Y'all got a dressing room in the middle of the desert? Dubai really is lit as fuck," Tiffany spat again.

"Can we get going please? All of this sand is making me itchy," Summer complained as the guide continued.

Memori walked back over towards her friends, and the instructor began to give the final instructions on how to brake and accelerate on the machines.

"We have one for you too," the instructor said, motioning for me to follow the group. I shook my head no, but the group of women urged me to come join them.

As much as I tried to decline, I eventually gave in to the peer pressure. We made our way over the hills and rode around for about twenty minutes before we got to the destination that the man had led us to. In the middle of the desert was a giant photography station set up with a sign that read, *Welcome to the Flying Dress.*

The ladies looked in astonishment as they had only heard about the attraction but didn't have it planned for themselves. Our entire group stopped our ATVs and made our way down to see what the hype was about.

The instructor led the ladies to a chest that was filled with different color dress garments and pointed them in the direction of where they could change. Each lady chose their dress color, and they headed to get dressed.

Upon their return, each of them looked elegant, but Memori stood out. She wore a red dress that hugged every curve imaginable on her body. I watched as each of them took their turn taking pictures while the others snapped photos with their phones. As Tiffany finished her photo shoot first, she walked over to me.

"That dress looks good then a motherfucker on my girl, huh?" she questioned.

I laughed and slightly blushed but shook my head yes.

"Listen, I can tell you're feeling her. The way you keep staring at her, it's obvious, but she's in a vulnerable place right now. She enjoys your company. So, while we're here, keep being genuine to her and let her know that there are some guys left in this world who value women. I know that the chances of you guys getting to know one another once we leave is slim to none, but if she's going to waste time while we're here with you, do the right thing. Don't hurt her, because I don't mind being left behind to rot in a jail cell."

I turned my head and looked directly into her eyes.

"You have my word that nothing will happen to your friend while I'm around. As a matter of fact, I've got all of y'all as long as you all are here."

She extended her fist and awaited mine to bump hers.

"My man," she stated as I did so. "Now look, you didn't hear it from me, but your boy Aquanis may need a couple days to recover. I put it on his ass."

I looked down at her with wide eyes, trying to read between the lines.

"Yeah, it's exactly what you think."

She started swaying her hips from side to side, and I burst out into laughter.

Two of the other women completed their shoots in the process of Tiffany and I talking, and Memori was last but certainly not least.

"Damn," I said out loud, thinking that I was containing that thought in my head.

"Why don't you go out there and take a picture or two with her? You ain't her man, but you have the red shirt on, and it wouldn't be a bad look. You not too bad looking of a dude."

I tried to decline, but the group once again pressured me into the situation. The pushed me out in front of the cameraman, towards Memori.

"What are you doing?" she questioned as I made my way over to her.

"If I knew right now, I would tell you, but your friends are persistent in making sure that this picture is taken, so here I am."

The cameraman gave instructions on how we should have been positioned, and we did as he commanded.

"On three, I want you to lift her into the air."

I looked at Memori, and she looked at me. Before we had the chance to agree or disagree, the cameraman said three. I elevated her into the air and looked towards the camera.

"The perfect photo," he stated as I sat her back onto the sand.

Memori and I locked eyes for a moment before we headed back to the area, where the girls needed to change back into their attire. Once they'd changed, we were back in the sprinter, heading towards our next destination.

"Hey, Sy'Cotic is it?" Summer stated a I looked back at her through the rearview. "Listen, I know you want to show us Dubai, but I'm going to be honest, after the ATV, all I want to do is go take a shower, get a drink, and hit the beach."

That seemed to be the consensus with the group.

"If that's what you ladies would like to do, I'll phone the aquarium and cancel your tour."

Memori was the only objection to the hotel.

"Look y'all, we could have stayed at home. Besides, we are literally going to go shower, just to get back into more sand. That makes no sense. The beach isn't going anywhere, but we get one chance to see what their Aquarium has to offer."

There was no change in the way that the other three ladies felt.

"Look girl, I love you, but I need to go wash my lady parts. You can go to the aquarium with the fish, but I'm going to sit by the ocean and tan."

It seemed as if the group had made their final decision, and back to the resort we started.

"You can take them back. Even if it's just me, I'd like to go to the Aquarium."

I smiled at Memori from the rearview, and she smiled back.

Parking in the front of the resort, I walked around to let the ladies who wanted to stay, out. Summer and Monica were the first two out as Tiffany and Memori spent a moment talking.

"I need to go handle that situation upstairs. I'll see you when you get back. Don't worry, my man and I here have talked; he's going to take good care of you."

I looked down at the ground and smirked as I helped Tiffany out of the sprinter.

"You have a way with the ladies, I see. It's not easy to get on her good side, so I'm impressed."

"It's the smile," I responded as I closed the door. Tiffany remained outside until she was sure that her friend was safe.

"Remember what I said, Sy'Cotic. Please don't fuck up with my friend. She will tell me, and if you do anything that pisses her off or hurts her, I'll cut your boy's dick off, get it stuffed, and use it as a dildo to fuck you in the ass."

"Wow. You are something else, but I got you."

I walked around to the driver door of the sprinter and got in. I rolled the passenger side window down and caught Tiffany's attention before she walked in.

"Aye, Tiffany! Tell Aquanis I said what's up and thank him for me."

She threw her hand up in the air, acknowledging what I'd just said, and Memori and I set off to the Aquarium.

We didn't spend a lot of time talking at the Aquarium; it was mostly just enjoying one another's company. Hell, honestly, I was just as impressed with the facility as she was. I'd been in Dubai for several years, and this was my first time stepping foot into the building. The deeper we got into the Aquarium, the darker it seemed to get. It was obvious that Memori had a slight fear of the dark because she would walk closer to me the darker a room got.

Once we were on the bottom floor the Aquarium, there was one small blue crack of light that seeped through. She was damn near in my skin as I held her close to me.

"You know that I'm not going to let anything happen to you."

She looked up at me, and it was almost as if time stood still. I leaned down and before I knew it, my lips were locked with hers. She pushed away from me once again, but this time, I pulled her back in. I wasn't going to allow her to deny what she was feeling. She embraced me, and we shared another kiss. Her knees got weak as she began to damn near melt in my arms.

"We need to go. We've got to go," she repeated a couple times.

Our tour of the aquarium had come to an end, and before I knew it, we were back in the sprinter, heading back to the resort. I kept my eyes on her from the rearview mirror. I watched her squirm in her seat uncomfortably, trying to adjust herself. I was for certain that she hadn't been as wet as she was in that moment for quite some time. She caught me looking at her and quickly put her head down.

As we arrived at the resort, she didn't wait for me to open the door. She did it herself and ran towards the beach to find her girls.

"Memori!" I yelled upon death ears.

I followed behind her, going towards the beach as well. Once outside, she'd found all her friends in the water. She rushed over to them. She and Tiffany exchanged words. Not too soon after, Tiffany motioned for me to come over. I walked over to the edge of the water, taking my shoes off. She motioned for me to come deeper into the water, and I obliged. I removed my shoes, then my shirt, before removing my khaki shorts. I was down to my boxers and walked out to the water.

"Listen, ok?" Tiffany stated as I approached. "Are you even real? You built like a damn transformer and I'm not about to even mention that fucking garden hose you have tucked in them boxers."

I watched as Memori slapped her on the arm as she peeked over her shoulder to see before fading back deeper into the ocean.

"Shit, yeah, listen, man. I don't know what you did to my girl, but man, I told you not to hurt her."

"I haven't done anything to hurt her."

"It's just you, bro. You exude this energy, and she isn't built for that."

I was frustrated by the words I was hearing from Tiffany. I felt as if Memori had something she needed to say, and she should have been woman enough to say it to me.

"I made you a promise, and I plan to keep it, Tiffany, but I won't stand here and get lectured. Memori is a grown ass woman. If she has something to say, she should come say it to me."

Memori faded further back into the water, and I threw my hands up in disbelief.

"I'm going to my room. I'll be in 1232 whenever she's ready to stop this childish shit. We shared a kiss, and now suddenly, I'm the bad guy."

I returned to the land, gathered my belongings, and headed back inside.

Chapter 11

Memori

You about one dirty bitch you know that?

-Nigel

I knew that I couldn't trust yo trifling ass but man I know the truth now.

– Nigel

Confused by the messages that I'd just received from my husband, I attempted to dial out to him, but the call failed twice.

What did I do now Nigel? I've been with the girls all day. I don't understand what the issue is.

-Memori

My message failed to send, and I sat there, dumbfounded. I asked Tiffany to use her phone, but she declined. She sat on the couch next to me and took my phone out of my hand. She read the text messages from Nigel and became livid.

"See, this is the problem. Stop feeding into the shit he's trying to get you to feed into. You're better than this."

She was right. I was better than the shit I was tolerating from him. In this instance, however, I was confused as to what sparked his outrage.

"I don't even know what I did this time."

"Memori, fuck what you did. Fuck him. He ain't good for

you. To be real, you need to fix the shit that's right here in front of you."

I was confused by her statement, but she got up from her seat and walked over to my roses and plucked one out.

"You need to go see him and apologize," Tiffany commanded as we smelled the flower.

"I don't know what to say to him." I looked up towards the ceiling and thought of what I could possibly say, but nothing came to mind. "You should come with me. I don't trust myself alone with him. I think I may say the wrong thing and piss him off, or worse. I might kiss him again."

Tiffany was growing frustrated. I could tell by her breathing pattern and the way that she clasped her fists into one another.

"I don't give a damn. He was right, and you were wrong this time. That man did nothing to put you in harm's way or hurt you, yet, you're making him out to be a monster because of your own insecurity. You can handle yourself. Set your boundaries and find a way to talk to him. Call him."

I pondered on her words, and it was the least I could do. The only issue was that I didn't have a number to reach him.

"I can't call him. I don't have a number for him."

"Well, I suggest you get your ass to room 1238 and see him face to face. You not about to keep dealing with this shit that's coming through your phone, as a matter of fact."

She took my phone and tossed it into her bedroom.

"You can have it back when you get back. If Nigel calls, I'll deal with him this time. Go apologize to that man, now."

I'd never seen Tiffany this riled up about a stranger. After several minutes of me going back and forth with myself outside of the suite's door, I made my way to the elevator. I pressed the button for twelfth floor and proceeded down the hallway to the corner apartment.

I knocked on the door hesitantly. He answered with his shirt off and immediately, my pussy started oozing for him.

"What's up?" he questioned with sweat beads over his body.

"I need to talk to you," I mentioned.

"I'm not with the games, Memori. Either we're going to talk like adults, or you can go ahead and head back down to your girls."

"I'm here to talk."

He invited me in, and his place smelled like a little piece of heaven. Everything in it was black, white, and chrome. I looked around as he escorted me over to his couch. As I sat down, he walked over to the desk area and sat on the rolling chair.

"So, what's up?"

"I like your place."

"Thank you," he replied.

There was a minute's worth of silence before he spoke again. "So, are we going to talk, or are we gone play the quiet game? If we're going to do that, let me know so that I can get back to my work out."

I placed my hands in one another and looked at them.

"Why me, Sy'Cotic? Of all the women in this resort, why attempt to attach and attract yourself to me?"

"Lift your head up when you speak to me."

I did as he asked, and he continued. "For that reason, right there. There's something about the look in your eyes that I can't resist. I see beyond the physical with you. I see the need that you have, and I want to help fill it. It's in your walk, your talk, that smile." He pulled his chair over towards the couch so that he could get a better look at me. "I know that you were apprehensive about the kiss earlier, but that wasn't my way of being aggressive in the situation. It was me fulfilling a desire that you felt just as much as I did. I need you to learn not to run from those desires. Run towards them. Every time something good comes along for you, you run from it because you're afraid of the what if factor. Live in the moment, Memori. Life is a sequence of short events that you can either make last a moment or make last a lifetime."

He didn't have to say another word. I placed both of my hands on his face and kissed him gently.

"I want this moment. Don't talk anymore. Let me have my moment."

The fire in our eyes danced as we stared affectionately back at one another. He took me by the hand and led me into his bedroom.

"Are you sure this is what you want?"

I shook my head yes; I was living in the moment, as he stated. I disregarded all other thoughts that quite frankly would have changed my mind. His touch was gentle. He took his time learning my body, caressing my curves slowly, passionately. He kissed my shoulder blades as he undressed me.

"There's no rush to this fairy tale. I got you."

I let out a moan as his fingers trailed my spine. I was becoming weaker by the moment as he worked his magic on me. I stood before him, completely naked and for once, I felt like I was noticed. I was his canvas, and he used his tongue to paint me ever so softly.

"You're safe in my arms."

He pushed me back on the bed and placed both of my legs on his shoulders. After kissing and sucking my inner thigh, he moved over to my pussy. He parted my lips with his tongue and began circling my clit as it were playing duck duck goose. Every time he gently sucked on my clit, my pussy oozed more nectar for him, and he wasn't a man who'd let it go to waste. He allowed it to drip down to my ass crack before he took his tongue and licked it back up. After having the appetizer and cumming a couple times, my pussy was screaming for the entrée. He stood to his feet and released every bit of ten inches. I wanted to run, but my body wouldn't allow me to. I was prepared for whatever damage there was to come from him.

"Relax. No regrets."

He came up and stuck his tongue into my mouth, relaxing me.

"No regrets," I reiterated to him. It was a simple phrase, yet it held so much weight.

His throbbing dick entered me, and it felt like every fiber of my being went into shock. I'd never felt anything this big. It was so painful, yet so pleasurable. As much as I wanted him to pull out, I wanted him to go just as deep. My moans intensified and so did the depth of his stroke.

"Ohhhhh, shit!" I cried out, feeling him fill my body up. I wasn't going to last long. I could feel my orgasm on the brink of pushing through, but his dick was so massive, it wasn't letting me release it. He began to talk to me, and that made this so much worse for me.

"Look at me in my eyes."

I did as he commanded, and he continued to destroy my pussy.

"You gone cum on this dick, baby?"

"Yes," I responded with tears flowing down my eyes.

"I need you, Memori," he stated, forcing another inch of his dick into me.

The tears flowed harder as I took him into me.

"I need you to cum for me."

His stroke intensified as he began to find a pounding rhythm.

"Oh, fuck!" I cried out. I placed my hand on his torso, attempting to hold him back, but he moved my hand downward. He made me grab the shaft of his dick. I was so wet and had creamed so much on his dick that I was almost embarrassed. He continued stroking through my hand deeper into my pussy.

I couldn't take it anymore, and before I knew it, my pussy had ejected his dick, and I was flopping around in the bed like a fish out of water, releasing fluids everywhere. Never, and I mean never, in my life had I released so much fluid let alone squirted. Yet, this man managed to make me and hadn't nutted himself.

I wasn't built for this. He was ready to get back into me, but I needed a moment to recuperate. His dick was standing just as strong and hard as it was when he first entered me. He leaned down and kissed my chest.

"Listen, I got you," he whispered. "Turn over. Lay on your stomach."

It took me a second, but I did just as he asked. He adjusted my body to his liking and in an instant, I felt that pleasurable sensation enter my body once more. He took his hands, reached around me, and played with my clit as he took long, slow, deliberately deep strokes in my pussy. It was like the longer the stroke, the more my pussy wanted in. I'd taken enough of him in; I could feel his balls slapping against my clit as he continued fingering it. With my head face down in the covers, I started to throw my body back onto him. I wanted to see how far I could go before I needed to quit. He began to moan as I began taking more of him, allowing whimpers of pleasurable pain and passion to escape my lips. My tears rolled as I clenched the sheets biting into them with with every powerful stroke he took. I didn't know if my pussy or my eyes soaked the sheets more, but I refused to stop until he released. He removed his hand from my clit and put both hands on my waist. Him taking turns with his hands slapping my ass sent me into overdrive and had me on the brink of another explosion.

"Cum on this dick, Memori... Cum on daddy dick... Let me get that shit, baby girl." My lungs lost air for a second, and before I knew it, my pussy had a death grip on his dick, and I was shaking.

I'd let out a barrage of curse words as he remained as deep as my pussy would allow him as he released himself. He even came sexy. He had a bear's growl as he released himself. As his dick began to soften, my pussy finally relaxed enough to release him. He crawled up into the bed next to me. I placed my head on top of his chest and listened to his heartbeat. The two of us laid there in that moment, together in total bliss.

Chapter 12

Memori

I'd fallen asleep at Sy'Cotic's place and completely lost track of time. He was still fast asleep when I gathered my belongings and left. I snuck back into my suite, but Tiffany was up and met me.

"Well, did you have fun?" she questioned, noticing that I wasn't as put together as I was the night before. I walked into my room and laid down, trying to get comfortable. My body was sore as hell, and my pussy still felt like Sy'Cotic was in it. Tiffany walked into my room, tossing me my phone.

"That shit's been going crazy. I don't know whose been blowing you up, but there you go," she mentioned, walking back towards her room. I opened my phone and noticed several disrespectful comments directed my way.

"Memori, calm down," I said to myself as rational thinking took over me. "Take a deep breath, girl. As much fucked up shit as that man has done to you, this is his karma. You've done nothing wrong."

I was hyperventilating after seeing and reading the words from Nigel. The thought of what I'd just done began to weigh heavy as I watched the video Nigel sent me. I had never been with another man until now. Hell, I hadn't even had thoughts of another man, yet here I was, out, being a full-blown adulterer according to the clip sent to me. I started hitting myself in the head.

Tiffany overheard the blows and rushed back into my room. When she returned, I looked like I had been in a full hurricane by the face.

"I need Sincere. I need to talk to him."

She sat next to me on the bed and began to console me.

"Memori, what's wrong? What just happened?" she questioned.

I need you now. It's an emergency

-Memori

Please do what you must to get me on the schedule today

-Memori

"How could I be so stupid?" I thought out loud as I began to cry harder. As much as I enjoyed my time with Sy'Cotic, I was in the wrong. My husband didn't deserve my betrayal at all. Even though he had his flaws, he didn't deserve it.

Hey, I'm pretty booked today. But I will try my best to squeeze you in. Be on the lookout for my call. -S.V.

I placed my phone on the bed and began to cry harder. Tiffany sat right by my side through it all.

"Memori, breathe. You're going to make yourself pass out. What's wrong, love?"

"Me, I'm what's wrong. I'm such a fucking idiot."

Tiffany looked at me confused because that wasn't the tune that I was singing the day before.

"What changed? What happened?" she questioned.

I opened my phone and scrolled to the text message thread. Nigel sent me a video of Sy'Cotic and me taking pictures during the beach trip. He'd screen recorded Summer's Instagram story.

"I cheated, Tiffany. I've never cheated. No matter how many times he's done me wrong, I've never stooped this low, and he knows. I'm sure of it."

Tiffany wiped a tear from me eye and moved my face to look at hers.

"Look at me. Usually, I would go down this emotional rollercoaster with you, but I'm not. You did something for you for once. Was it right? Maybe not, but you lived. You experienced something outside of the four walls that you've been accustomed to for so long. For that, I'm proud of you."

She kissed my cheek and continued. "Nigel ain't shit; we both know that. You stay out of love. As you can see, the love is running out, and you loving him is real one sided. You needed this. As wrong as it may be, you did."

It was hard for me to hear her words. She was condoning my actions, yet I was still broken and torn behind it. As much as she was attempting to help me get through it, I needed to speak to Sincere.

Tiffany sat with me another twenty minutes or so, calming my nerves and getting me to a point where I was able to function without tears. She called down to room service and ordered us something to drink to take the edge off.

"You need to get out of this room."

"I don't want to leave, Tiffany. I'm scared that if I do, I'll run into him."

"You can't be scared of that man; he's done nothing wrong."

"You don't understand. He touched me in ways that I never knew were imaginable. He makes me weak. He makes my body crave him. I've never craved a man while he was inside of me. I can't shake him, and I think he knows that."

"Yeah, girl, you need some fresh air. Come on, let's at least look at the beach from the balcony."

I agreed to do that. There was a slight breeze, but the heat remained in place. I stood close to the balcony's edge, looking below.

"Bitch, back yo' ass up. You ain't about to do that bullshit to me," Tiffany stated, jumping up from her seat, pulling my shirt. "Nope, on my watch."

As I was flung backwards into the chair that was sitting behind me, she circled around, stood in front of me, and slapped me.

"I'm not about to lose you. Shake this shit off!" she barked.

With a stung face, I sat in shock from the slap.

"I wasn't gone jump, Tiffany. I just needed some fresh air. This was your idea, remember?"

"Well, I'm sorry for slapping the shit out of you, but there's plenty of good air from that seat, so sit yo' ass down."

I did exactly that, still trying to comprehend what had just happened. I collected my thoughts and feelings. As I did, my phone began to ring. It was a FaceTime from Sincere.

"Good morning, Memori, or afternoon, in your case," he stated as he started the call.

He noticed me rubbing my face and the red mark that was left there.

"Memori, is everything ok?" he questioned.

"Yes, everything is ok."

"She's fine, doc," Tiffany spat in the background. "I thought she lost her mind for a second, so I smacked some sense into her ass."

"Hello, Tiffany," Sincere stated, overhearing her voice.

"I'm going to let y'all talk. Keep yo' ass in that seat, or I'm coming back with the back hand this time," Tiffany stated, motioning her hand from front to back.

She went into the suite and closed the door behind her.

"Your girl is something else," Sincere mentioned.

"She is, but I need her to keep me straight sometimes."

"So, what's going on?" he questioned once more.

"I don't even know where to start. So, I took your advice and have truly been enjoying my trip out here, but I fucked up."

"What do you mean by you fucked up? Did you hurt someone, Memori? Are you thinking of hurting yourself?"

"I haven't hurt anyone yet," I responded with tears in my eyes. "I don't know."

"Hey, calm down, relax. Let's talk through this. What happened?"

"I met a guy. He was sweet, assertive, charming, and nice. He reminded me of you a lot."

Sincere looked over at his fiancée, and I could hear her cough in the background.

"Not in a sexual way. Not in those words, but appearance-wise, he favors you."

She coughed again.

"Go ahead. Please continue," he stated.

"Sy'Cotic and I hit it off after I got into a disagreement with Nigel. I was vulnerable. I gave in, and I cheated on my husband," I continued explaining through teary eyes and mumbled speech.

Sincere placed his hand over his mouth, thinking on what he

should say to me.

"What did you say this guy's name was?"

"Sy'Cotic. Sy'Cotic Baptiste. Why?"

His eyes got wide like he'd seen a ghost. He then went away from the camera before reappearing.

"Ok, Memori. It's not the end of the world; it's going to be ok. I'm not telling you that I'm condoning your actions, but I do want you to know that you can work through this."

"What do I do?" I asked him, concerned about what was next to come.

"Just process what you're going through but don't beat yourself up. What's done is done; you can't change it. It happened." He paused for a minute then cleared his throat. "As for this mystery man. You stated that he favored me. What exactly does he look like? Do you have a picture?"

"Yes." I scrolled Instagram and sent him the video of the two of us. "Feature-wise, you all favor one another a lot. He might be a shade darker. I don't know if you can see his face too good in the video that I just sent over."

He looked towards his fiancée and mumbled something.

"Did he happen to tell you any personal information, like where he's from or how he ended up in Dubai?"

"He didn't give me the details as to how he got here. He just kept avoiding the question. He did say something about business brought him over. However, he told me that he was from South Florida. Oh, and he knew Creole. He's mixed with Haitian."

"Thank you." Sincere got quiet once more. "If you get the chance, and in no way am I attempting to put you in an uncomfortable situation, but if see him again, will you snap a better picture of him and send it to me?" His request was awkward, but I agreed to do it. "When you return to the states, I need to see you in my office immediately."

Again, I shook my head in agreeance.

"Is there anything else that you would like to get off your chest?"

"I don't think so. Is there anything that you would like to get off yours? You seem mighty interested in this guy."

He coughed, looked at his fiancée, and motioned for her to keep quiet.

"I just want to make sure I have the face of the guy if anything happens to you. I think that you've been through and suffered enough without adding any more to it."

The call disconnected, and I was left still in a rather weird space after talking to Sincere.

Tiffany got up from the couch, noticing that I was off the phone.

"You feeling better now?" she asked.

I shook my head no. I was more confused now than I had been. Something wasn't adding up, and I felt like there was more that Sincere wanted to tell me; he just couldn't. As much as I didn't want to see Sy'Cotic, I knew that I needed to in order to get some clarity.

Chapter 13

Sy'Cotic

After the time spent with Memori, I couldn't get her off my mind. There was no one that had ever garnered my thoughts the way that she had. Today was her last day in Dubai, and I wanted to attempt to steal a little bit of her time before she and her friends left to go back to the states. I set up a brunch date for the girls, hoping to at least see her before she left. I arranged for Aquanis to go get them from their suites and meet me us downstairs. He did as he was asked, and the group of ladies made their way down to the area.

I'd taken the liberty of completely shutting down one of the restaurants so that they could enjoy their last meal here in Dubai. As they entered, my gesture didn't go unnoticed. Each of them was taken aback by the set up. Summer and Monica entered first with their phones out, as Tiffany and Memori followed behind, conversing with one another as they usually did. As Memori entered, I gently reached out and grabbed her arm.

"Good morning," I stated.

She stopped in her tracks and gave me her attention.

"Good morning."

She tried to avoid eyes contact, but I wouldn't allow it. I lifted her head and looked into her eyes. They were red and still slightly puffy.

"Everything ok?"

She shook her head yes. "Everything will be fine. Can we go talk for a second?"

I looked back into the restaurant as her friends got settled in. She and I began to walk towards a sitting area in the lobby.

"What's on your mind, beautiful?" I questioned, running my fingers over her face.

She placed her hand on top of mine and began to speak.

"I don't regret anything that we did here, but I know that reality is about to set back in. I appreciate you for making me feel wanted, for making me feel appreciated. For that, I can never repay you."

It felt like a scene in a movie as the two of us conversed. She was right; our fairy tale was coming to an end, and reality was about to hit us both hard.

"Look, I know that you're about to go back home. Just promise me that you won't forget me. I'd love for us to remain distant friends some way, somehow."

"I don't know if that's the best idea, but I'm taking your lead here and living in the moment. We will try to make it work. I would say that I want you to come visit the states, but that may be a really bad idea."

I shook my head in agreement. That idea was beyond bad for several reasons on both of our ends.

"If I don't make it to the states, you can always come back out here, and we can pick up where we left off." I pulled her in close to me and just held her against my chest. I kissed the top of her forehead before I lifted her chin to kiss her lips. Our kiss lasted no longer than a second but would be a memory that was lasted an eternity.

"I guess I got the answer to my question."

She looked at me confused as we began to walk back over to her friends.

"I guess the Memori that I bring out is a good one. I got to see the best of you in a dark time in your life. So, thank you for that."

She pulled out her phone and opened the camera app on it. She took a picture of the two of us and then handed it to me.

"I just don't want to forget how free and happy I am right now in this moment with you. When I get home, there's a lot that I need to unravel, but I want to at least be able to find you when I need to talk."

I entered my contact information into her phone and allowed her to leave me. She smiled and headed into the restaurant to eat with her friends.

As the ladies ate, I pulled Aquanis away from Tiffany for a moment to speak to him.

"Make sure nothing goes wrong at the airport. Get them where they need to be safely. I appreciate you, my man. When you get back, though, we're going to talk about that sickness you had."

I punched him in the shoulder and sent him on his way. An hour or so passed, and I'd sent the ladies into the sprinter. Just as they were pulling off, my phone went off. It was a request on Instagram. I looked at it and noticed that it was Memori. Her profile name was *EverlastingMemori*. I couldn't do anything but laugh at it. It was ironic yet fitting for the woman she was.

Chapter 14

Memori

Reality set in as our flight touched down. I hated that vacation was over, knowing the shit show that I was about to walk into. I expected Nigel to be at the airport to greet me, however, he was nowhere to be found and wasn't answering his phone.

I'm back home. Can you come get me from the airport please? We can talk and get whatever animosity there is between us out the way. -Memori

He didn't respond to my text nor did his phone give me the notification that it had been read. He must have been sleep. I decided to hitch a ride with Tiffany, and she dropped me off at home. I noticed that my car hadn't moved since I'd left. The window was still missing, and there was water on the inside from where it had rained.

"This nigga, man," I said out loud, furious that he hadn't done as he'd said and gotten my shit fixed.

I didn't see his car in the driveway as I entered the house. It was cold. It didn't feel like a happy home. I took my bags to our bedroom and dropped them at the foot of the bed. I sat down and opened my phone, looking at the photo of Sy'Cotic and me. I sent him a direct message on Instagram, letting him know that I'd made it back to the states. I followed that up by reaching out to Sincere.

I've made it back to the states. Just wanted to give you a heads

up.

-Memori

I know that you may need some time to unwind, but if you can make it to my office, I will clear my schedule. I need to see you.

-S.V.

Something told me that I was about to get some answers to the questions that were formulating about his mysterious request into Sy'Cotic.

I can be there in an hour.

-Memori

I attempted to call Nigel twice more and got the voicemail both times. I checked his location on my phone and noticed that he was alive because the pin was moving. He was still on fuck shit. I went into the bathroom and freshened up from the long flight then prepared to go to my therapist's office.

Once I arrived at the office, upon entering the building, I was met with a side eye from his assistant, Shianne.

"Good afternoon. He's in there waiting for you."

She'd never been as cold as she was being to me. I blew it off and headed into his office. Dr. Valentino was sitting with his feet on top of his desk, crossed on top of one another. He was flipping through a couple of files and some photos.

"Memori," he stated, popping up from his seat to come over to greet me. He embraced me with a hug and pulled my seat out for me. He sat on the top of his desk and began to ask me questions.

"So how was the trip, outside of the incident?"

"It was great," I replied. "I was able to relax, write in my journal, and try to find a part of me that I didn't know was still there."

"Excellent," he replied. "No other mishaps that I should know about?"

I shook my head no, and my phone began to buzz in my pocket. It was Nigel.

"Hold off before you answer that," he stated. He cleared his throat and sat in his chair. "Were you able to get a better picture of Sy'Cotic for me?"

I shook my head yes, opened my camera gallery, and showed him the picture. His eyes got wide, and he paged Shianne to come into his office. Not too long after, she was standing right next to him, looking at the photo. He lifted the files that he was looking at and placed the phone side by side.

"Do you think so?" he questioned, looking up at his assistant.

"With the time that's passed, it could be."

I was confused about the conversation that the two of them were having and wanted some answers.

"So, what's going on right here?" I questioned.

Dr. Valentino looked at me and cleared his throat. He handed me the files with the photo and began to explain.

"For years, I've been looking for someone I thought might have been dead. Ever since I got out of jail and rehabilitated my life, I've been looking for him. Month in and month out, my mother's estate has been dropping funds into an offshore account that I knew very little about. I'd always assumed that it was either for my uncle, who went missing after my arrest, but without ever hearing from him, I'd assumed the worst. It was like he just vanished into thin air. My mother told me that there was a shoot out shortly after I got apprehended and that an officer was killed. I'd always thought the worst and assumed that my uncle was taken from us in the same manner."

Still attempting to grasp what was going on, I continued to listen.

"When you told me that you'd met a Haitian man with the name Sy'Cotic Baptiste, it struck me. I don't know how many men have that name with the same origin. My real name is Sincere Baptiste, and I think you found my brother for me. He was with my uncle and myself that night, but he went in an opposite direction, never to be heard from again."

"Wait... Wait...Wait... so, you think Sy'Cotic is your brother?"

"Yes, look at the resemblance between him as a grown man and the photo of us when we first moved to Louisiana. You stated yourself that his looks favor mine. Look at his photo next to my face."

"Just because y'all look alike doesn't mean that y'all are brothers. Hell, it doesn't mean that y'all are related. A lot of people have doppelgängers. Besides, that man has been on the other side of the world, living his best life. He owns an entire company over there."

He flipped the pages on the file and showed me a statement from his mother's estate.

"Is that the name of the company?"

I looked at the name, and sure enough, the documentation said SY'CO.

"My mother knew about my brother's whereabouts and hid that from me. I need to talk to him. Is there any information that you can give me to contact him?"

It was all too much for me to process. I opened my Instagram and gave him the name of Sy'Cotic's private profile name.

"This is more than enough. Thank you so much, Memori."

My phone began to buzz as I took it back from Dr. Valentino. It wasn't a call or text; it was Nigel's location pinging. I looked at it and noticed the house that he'd stopped at.

"That's weird," I thought out loud.

Dr. Valentino and his assistant were going back and forth on how to proceed with the information they were just given.

"Hey, are we all good here? I need to go."

He shook his head yes, and the two of them escorted me towards the exit. I got into my car and entered the location in my GPS. I was hoping and praying that Nigel wasn't where I thought he was because if he was, the only thing that was going to be able to help him was God himself.

As I approached the house, I noticed his car outside. Too many thoughts began to come to my mind as I became infuriated. It was starting to make sense. The late-night call, the hearts under the Instagram post, him coming at my neck about the Instagram video.

I pulled my pistol from beneath my front seat and tucked it in my waist before walking up to the door. I could hear laughter as I got closer. I knocked on the door. The laughter ceased, and the door swung open.

"Memori," Summer's eyes got as wide as they could. Behind her stood Nigel, adjusting his belt buckle.

Before I knew it, I'd hit Summer's ass square in her eyes and pulled the pistol from my waist.

"You got me fucked up, nigga," I mentioned, pointing the pistol towards Nigel's direction. "And you bitch! You been smiling in my face and fucking my nigga behind my back." I kicked her in her stomach repeatedly then let off several shots.

BANG… BANG… BANG…

WANT TO INTERACT WITH T'ANN MARIE & HER TEAM? JOIN OUR READERS GROUPS ON FACEBOOK!

T'ANN MARIE PRESENTS: GRANDMA'S HOUSE | Facebook

T'ANN MARIE PRESENTS: GRANDMA'S HOUSE 2.0 | Facebook

WIN PRIZES, BE APART OF LIVE BOOK DISCUSSIONS & MORE!

Join Our Mailing List:

http://eepurl.com/gU81k5

TMP
TANN MARIE PRESENTS
is now accepting submissions in the following genres

URBAN FICTION * URBAN ROMANCE
STREET LIT * URBAN PARANORMAL
INTERRACIAL ROMANCE

for consideration, please email the first 5 chapters of your manuscript to:

TANNMARIESUBS@GMAIL.COM